No Angels

Andrea Jenelle

To every reader who believes in second
chances.

Contents

Prologue

Bianca

O￼UR MOMS HAVE BEEN *best friends since the second grade.*

He's been pulling my braids and annoying me since we were in the second grade.

He's the one that dared me to ride my bike down Sanderson Hill when I was ten.

I broke my arm.

He's the one that dared me to go in the creepy, abandoned house on the edge of town when we were thirteen.

I got locked in the cellar.

Today we both exited left off that stage and said hello to being adults.

Now we're standing in the middle of a hay-field beneath the glow of the full moon and he's daring me to kiss him. I have good reason to be scared of what will happen if I do.

But there's a reason he dares me and there's a reason I take every single dare to heart.

"Come on, Bumble Bee. What are you afraid of?"

He's using the nickname he gave me when we were seven. "I'm not afraid of anything. But you know I'm leaving, so why now?"

He cups my cheek in his hand and I when I look in his eyes, I can see the boy he was and the man he's becoming.

"Maybe I'm hoping my kiss will convince you to stay in Willow Creek instead of chasing the bright lights and the big city."

"Mike, you're my best friend. You've been my best friend my entire life. Even if every time you dare me it ends in disaster. If you wanted to be more than friends, why haven't you said something before now?"

Has he always felt this way? Why didn't he ask me to prom? Or homecoming? Why didn't he give the bouquet of wildflowers Angela Jenkins tossed in his face to me instead?

"I thought if I didn't say anything, I could pretend this would never happen. That you wouldn't leave."

"This is my dream. It's been my dream since I was Little Bo Peep in the spring recital when we were eight."

"Maybe I can come with you."

"Your family needs you here. And my mom needs somebody. She can't run her farm or the feed store all by herself. I'm counting on you to be my eyes and my ears. And you have a lacrosse scholarship. You can't leave all that behind to follow me. Especially when I might end up nothing more than a starving artist." I punch him in the stomach and my fist bounces off. "I've seen how much food you eat in one sitting."

"I still want to kiss you. Even if it's the first and last time."

"Fine. Do your worst, Callihan."

The soft contours of his lips are a revelation.

Why didn't I ask him for my first kiss when he carried me home from my bike accident or rescued me from the haunted house?

Without breaking the kiss, he tangles our fingers together and starts backing up. He leans against a stack of haybales and pulls me closer.

I drank almost an entire bottle of Boone's Farm and I can feel it fizzing all over my body. It's the first taste of wine I've ever had, and I figured I should celebrate both my graduation and the beginning of the new chapter I'm about to start.

His thumbs are callused because he's the lead snare in the marching band, and he skates them over the vertebra at the edge of my jeans. I feel the rough stroke over that tiny space of skin. A space that should be too small to leash the echo of his touch and transmute it like a lightning bolt to every single one of my nerve endings.

I place my hands against his chest and gently shove. I need to catch my breath and set the record straight about where he thinks this kiss is going.

"Callihan, I need a minute."

He lifts his head. "Take a minute, Cassidy. But that's all I'm letting you have. I need to store up memories so I won't miss you as much when you go."

Mike Callihan is the kind of guy who doesn't let on how he feels. I'm always teasing him about his poker face, and he's beaten me at every single high stakes card game we've played. If I was so essential to him, why didn't he tell me sooner?

"Mike, I never suspected you felt this way. It's too fast and too unexpected."

"It's just a kiss, Cassidy, not a marriage proposal."

"I know," I grumble into the tiny space between us as he drops his head again. Why didn't he tell me sooner? Would it have affected my decision to leave?

Something in my tone must be a red flag, because he tilts my face up and scrutinizes my expression. "That's not something you want, right?"

I shake my head. "Nope, just wish you'd kissed me sooner."

"I always thought you wanted to be nothing more than friends. It's funny," he says as he slides the pads of his fingers down the line of my throat. "We told each other every secret but the one that would have changed everything the most."

"You wish you'd kissed me sooner?"

"Hell, yeah," he mutters as he drops his mouth to mine again.

It's a long time before we come up for air.

Chapter One

Mike

Twenty years ago, Bianca Cassidy showed me the only angels I'll find here in Willow Creek have shredded wings and crumpled halos.

I can't believe she's back and I want to know why. When the mayor, Zane Reid introduced us, she just reached out her hand and said, "We already know each other. Long time no see, Mike."

I was too dumbstruck to reply with anything other than a curt nod.

But the first rehearsal is over, and the last angel in the choir just got picked up. I snag Bianca's arm and haul her behind the curtains in case there are any parents left to eavesdrop on what I need to say.

It smells like sawdust and lemon oil back here, and the motes I just stirred up when I brushed past the heavy velvet are swimming in little clouds. It's quiet and secluded and I can get the answers I need for my peace of mind.

"What are you doing here?" I ignore the crack at the end of my question that lets on how much I'm invested in her answer.

She left the morning after we graduated from Willow Creek High School and never looked back.

The morning after the kiss that turned my world upside down, she hopped on a bus to New York City. The kiss that made me feel like I'd just figured out how to start a fire, that rewired my brain, wasn't enough to change her mind. It wasn't enough to keep her in Willow Creek.

What I was offering her when I kissed her wasn't enough to hold her here, and I gave up on making her mine years ago.

I'm lying to myself, because I've been thinking about the kiss off and on since the day she left. I wonder if there's anything I could have done to change her mind. Like kissing her sooner. Like using my words to let her know how I felt the night before she was going to leave this place and never look back.

There were a couple of calls – but it was before cell phones were really a thing. One day I called because I wanted to hear her voice and ask if she'd be home for Christmas and it wasn't her who answered. The guy who picked up the phone told me she was in the shower and if I was that loser from back home I should just do myself a favor and stop calling because she was never going back to that podunk place. He said she al- ways laughed – and not in a nice way- when she talked about it and me.

So I never called again. I let her drift away.

I thought about her because there was an empty space where her smile used to be. For the first fifteen years, I couldn't stand the smell of strawberries.

When her mom was diagnosed with cancer the first time and she didn't come back, I stopped thinking about the Boone's Farm strawberry kiss and the way the freckles across her nose looked like the Sagittarius constellation by the end of summer. Because she'd grown into someone I didn't know. Nothing would have kept away the girl I knew. Not even a natural disaster.

I made myself forget the way she murmured my name when I cupped her nape in that hayfield and her voice was like cotton candy and hot fudge sundaes.

She's staring at me like I've offended her. But I need to know what she's doing here after all this time. Besides disrupting my life.

"Come on, Bianca. We both know you're not really here to shepherd around a bunch of rowdy five-year-old angels and herd cats so you can direct a mediocre town Christmas play. Why are you really here?"

"What do you mean, why am I here? And it's not going to be mediocre. It'll be the best Christmas pageant ever."

I crowd her against the half-built scaffolding. "I mean why are you here when you have a life in the city? You were a Broadway star and you left it all behind and came home to this mountain town in the middle of nowhere. I'm not buying your story. Adding this little escape to your resume won't do you any favors and we both know it."

She's flustered. Her cheeks are bright pink and her breaths whistle over my shoulder in rapid little puffs of distress.

"I'm here because my mom needed me here while she fights for remission."

"That's not the only reason. It's been over ten years since you even bothered to visit. I was the one who made sure she got the harvest in, fixed the roof on the barn and made sure she had kids to work at the feed store every summer. Now tell me what made you tuck your tail between your legs and come scurrying back here. According to your boyfriend you couldn't leave us all behind fast enough."

She narrows her eyes. Like I have no right to demand explanations.

"If I have other reasons for being here, you're not entitled to hear them. They're none of your business. And I don't have a boyfriend."

My heart irrationally kicks up at her admission. I wonder what happened to the douchebag that answered her phone all those years ago. Has he been out of the picture for a while? Has she had a string of boyfriends or is she serially monogamous like me?

I want to dip my head and smell the little crevice behind her ear. I need to know if she still smells like lilies of the valley.

I smother the urge and narrow my eyes right back.

She frowns and crosses her arms, rubbing her hands over her elbows.

When she bites her lip, I want to soothe it with my tongue.

"I know I was selfish. But Mom never asked me to come back. Every time I called she told me how proud she was of me. She always deflected the conversation away from her own worries."

"And you didn't push her for answers because your career was more important to you than your family. Or anyone else in Willow Creek."

I want to take back the bitter words. I don't want her to know how much I've missed her. She doesn't need to know that the strawberry-infused kiss I stole has haunted me for eighteen years. She doesn't need to know how many times I wished I could pick up the phone and tell the girl who used to be my best friend what was going on in my life.

"Trust me, I'm well aware how much everyone disapproves of me. I agree with them, so you don't need to keep rubbing dirt in my wounds."

"I'm not doing that. I just want you to know that the rest of us have been picking up the pieces of debris you left in your wake." Especially me.

She sighs and drops her arms. "Mom always told me she didn't want me to get stuck here."

"That's how you think of this place?" *That's how you think of me? As a way to trap you somewhere you don't really want to be?*

She shakes her head. "No. Not until we graduated. Even then, I didn't want to leave."

"Why didn't you want to leave?" Does she mean she didn't want to leave me? She didn't even tell me goodbye. "You were the star of every single play and your future was bright. You deserved the opportunity. Even if we were all sorry to see you leave and missed you."

"You missed me?"

I step away, so she won't see all those old feelings surfacing in my eyes. "Of course I did."

I missed her the way sailors miss red sunsets and soldiers miss peace.

She wedges her hand between us and rests it in the middle of my chest.

"I thought about the kiss a lot. It was a memory that kept me warm."

"Why didn't you leave me your number when you moved out of your first apartment?"

"Because I missed you and there was no room for you in my life then. But I thought about the kiss. Especially when the city was covered in a blanket of snow and I was banging my iron skillet against the radiator."

"Because the memory of our kiss kept you warm?"

She slowly shakes her head. "Nooo...," she drawls.

"Tell me why you thought about that kiss." My nails are digging into my palms. So I won't give into temptation again and touch her. She's not here to stay. Why would she be?

She lifts her chin and resolve floods her face. It's the same look she got every time I dared her when we were kids. "I thought about it because it was my first kiss. And I'd been wanting it for a really long time before you finally made your move."

I take a step closer, erasing my retreat. "How long?"

She bites her lip and I want to soothe it. "Since that weekend you tried to teach me to drive your old pickup truck."

I smile at the memory. "You almost tore out my transmission."

She wanted to learn to drive a stick so I offered to teach her. After we stalled out at a stoplight on the top of Harmar Hill, she panicked. We started rolling backward and I was shouting instructions and she was crying and red faced. When she finally managed to crank it again and floored it so we fishtailed when we took off, we both started laughing.

We were laughing so hard we couldn't see straight, and I motioned for her to pull over

at the Dairy Freeze. I bought us both waffle cones – vanilla for me and chocolate
with sprinkles for her.

She asked for a taste of mine and I asked
for a taste of hers. When I handed her
my cone and her raspberry pink tongue
snuck out and licked the melting vanilla,
I couldn't look away.

That's when it started for me. It probably
started way before that, but I didn't ac-
knowledge it. Some part of me knew she
was it for me the time she beat me in the
fifty-yard dash on field day in fifth grade.
But that ice cream cone was the thing that
brought it all home. It's when I knew I'd
never be the same.

"That's when it started for you too?"

"Yeah," she ruefully admits. "I thought you were going to ask me to the junior prom."

"I didn't."

She grimaces. "No. You asked Cindy Houlihan. And even though she was the head cheerleader and you were a gearhead instead of a football player, she said yes."

"And we were together until the day all of us graduated."

"The day you finally kissed me – after I'd already been waiting for two years and after I'd already made plans to leave. You waited too long. I wasn't going to stay – no matter how good the kiss was."

I step back. If she could walk away from all those memories, away from me after I kissed her, maybe she was never the girl I thought she was. Or the girl I wanted her to be.

And maybe the woman isn't for me either.

I give her a hard look and she glares right back. "Fine," I tell her.

When I walk away this time, I don't look back.

Chapter Two

Bianca

"Hey honey," Mom calls from her spot on the couch as I toe off my shoes.

"Hey Mom." She has chemo tomorrow, so I know she's taking it easy this evening so she can gather her strength. "I was going to make potato soup for dinner, is that okay?"

She yawns. "That sounds delicious. If I can't keep my eyes open, we'll have leftovers tomorrow."

"I saw Mike today. You never mentioned he was still here."

Mom sighs and makes her way into the kitchen. She slides an arm around my waist. "I didn't want to upset you. I always knew you wanted him to look at you as more than the neighbor kid with the braids hanging down her back."

She's always been able to see straight through me. "He was my crush all through high school. I thought he didn't see me that way until he kissed me the night before I left."

"Oh my. You've kept that secret close."

I shrug as I set the cutting board on the is-land. "It didn't mean anything. I was leaving and there was no point in dwelling on it."

"Bee," she chides. "I know you better than that. You purposely ghosted him didn't you?"

I grab a red onion and when I slice it, it's not the only thing that brings tears to my eyes. "I couldn't afford to let him get to me, Mom. Broadway was always my dream. We called each other every week at first, but when I moved into the apartment with Cheryl, we lost touch."

Cheryl was an understudy in the trenches with me and when I broke up with my first real boyfriend Greg because I found him in bed with our next-door neighbor, she made me move in with her. She's my best friend and the one that convinced me I needed a break to get my stride back. I'm in Willow Creek because of her.

"You two were inseparable growing up, so I bet today was awkward."

I snort. "That's one way to describe it."

"Was he angry?" She quietly asks.

"Yeah. But I think it's because I hurt him."

"Are you going to be able to work with him on the pageant without your past getting in the way?"

"I don't know, Mom. It'd be easier to just avoid him."

"You can't runaway from your history, Bee," she admonishes as she tugs the end of my ponytail.

I bite my lip and remind myself she's just trying to be helpful. "He made it crystal clear how much he resents me for leaving."

"I'm sure it doesn't help that he's the town heartthrob."

I shrug. "I hadn't noticed." I hope my flush is only under the skin.

"I can tell when my daughter is fibbing. Any woman with eyes can't help noticing that tall drink of water."

I playfully smack her arm. "Please don't tell me when you notice things like that."

She rolls her eyes and chuckles delightedly. "I'll never be too old to notice those things, but I promise not to talk about them *too* much."

Once we've had our soup and she's taken her medicine, I walk her to the bedroom on the main floor. It's a lot harder for her to navigate the steep staircase to the second story, and this is our compromise. It makes sense because the downstairs bedroom has a bath right across the hall. Getting her to agree to even this small concession felt like I was negotiating the assault on Normandy.

When she's burrowed beneath the mound of blankets, I drop a kiss on her forehead. "Sleep tight, Mom."

"You too," she murmurs. "And don't let the bedbugs bite. If they do, take a shoe and hit them 'til they're black and blue."

Her bedtime greeting takes me straight back to my childhood, when she and dad used to tuck me in. Before their divorce and all the uncertainty that followed.

"I'll do that," I tell her as I softly shut the door behind me.

I fall into my own bed, my thoughts racing. All the echoes of my childhood surround me. I'm lying on top of the same pink ruffled princess comforter and the walls are still plastered with pictures of my favorite emo bands. The owl finial Callihan gave me after he rescued me from the haunted house is resting on the white bookshelf in front of my battered copy of Anne of Green Gables.

I jump up and grab it, rubbing my thumb over the ears worn smooth by time. When I close my eyes I can still smell the crepe myrtle and feel the wet grass sliding over my ankles. I remember laughing up at him in the moonlight and the way the air was suddenly heavy between us. We were fourteen and it was the first time I realized I wanted to kiss him. I didn't get my wish until it was too late to do a course correction that would've upended all my other dreams.

Mike Callihan always knew how to get under my skin and mash down my buttons. He has no right to question the decisions I've made about my career. Then or now.

I can't believe Mom didn't tell me he stayed in Willow Creek or that he's the one who's been helping her with everything. There's a part of me that still feels guilty for leaving him behind. I didn't even say goodbye because he might have convinced me that next to him was where I'd always belonged.

Which is why I didn't say goodbye. I couldn't take that chance.

The reasons I left don't matter, because he's not the reason I'm back. My career is a train wreck and my mom is stubborn about staying here. I need to figure out how I'm going to get back in the spotlight and convince her to move to New York. I'm subletting my apartment, but it's a temporary solution.

———— ◆◇◆ ————

Tonight is the first big rehearsal and I'm kicking myself for agreeing to do this. Mom is on the town council and she begged me to produce and direct the town's Christmas pageant this year. When she told me I'd help stage *The Best Christmas Pageant Ever*, I couldn't turn her down. When I left Willow Creek, I was cast as the villain of the story, even though I was nothing like Imogene Herdman. You won't catch me smoking cigars in the bathroom, but I feel an affinity with her.

The aggressive knock on my office door startles me. The theatre is usually quiet until the kids start trickling in for evening practice around four.

"Come in," I call.

The burly ginger guy my mom pointed out as the new town sheriff pushes the door open.

This is unexpected and like it always did when I engineered an epic prank as a kid and had to face the consequences when I was caught, my stomach drops to my knees. "Can I help you, Sheriff?"

Is he here to run me out of town because of public opinion? My mom's a fixture in Willow Creek, and I've been fielding judgmental stares since I got back last week. The general consensus is I'm a terrible daughter and a despicable human being for letting her deal with her cancer alone. It wasn't all my choice – she reassured me that she had a network of support and I shouldn't worry. That she could easily find someone to ferry her back and forth from her appointments and sit with her after the chemo treatments.

"Ms. Cassidy, I have a favor to ask."

He's twisting his hat in his hands like he's nervous. This is a first, so I decide to put him out of his misery. "Okay. What is it?"

"I'd like to make participating on the pageant part of the public service requirement for the Donaldson twins."

"And you need my permission?"

His laugh is acerbic. "Not really, but I don't want to create animosity."

"Why would assigning them to me create animosity?"

He cocks his head. "I take it you haven't met them."

"No, but I wasn't exactly a field of daisies growing up. It can't be that bad."

"They teepeed town hall and put something in the fountain in the square that makes the water look like a blood bath. We caught them on the surveillance cameras."

I can't let on how impressed I am by their ingenuity or how badly I want to know how they managed it. "Why make the pageant part of their punishment?"

"Well, my fiancé Emma told me she thinks they could use some churching to learn proper manners, and maybe if they have a bunch of parts to memorize they won't have time to brew more mischief."

That never worked for me. It always seemed like the busier I was, the more trouble I managed to find. "I could use some shepherds."

"I'll have their mom bring them over after school today."

"I'll be here to show them the ropes, and I think Mike is working on the set this evening." He's been avoiding me like the plague since our close encounter behind the curtains four days ago, so I'm assuming he'll be here.

Sheriff Hayes nods again. "He's used to their antics. He can help you keep an eye on them."

The inclusion of the troublesome twins has me wondering how big their family is. What if there really is a clan like the Herdmans here in Willow Creek?

"Is it just the twins or will their siblings be joining them?"

The cop swipes his hand over his face. "Just the two of them, thank God. I don't think Willow Creek could handle more than that."

So I'll get just a taste of the Herdmans, not the full cohort. "We'll keep them in line. Maybe the play will teach them a lesson about the Christmas spirit."

He ruefully shakes his head. "Not likely. They've been pranking it around town since they were in kindergarten. Their mom has tried everything."

"Then I probably shouldn't tell you thank you. They sound like public enemy number one."

"You definitely shouldn't tell me thank you. You're going to cuss up a storm behind my back once you meet them."

⁓⊙⁓

The sheriff was right. The Donaldson twins are a menace. One of them already smeared peanut butter on the dressing room doorknob, and they've managed to make Mary and one of the angels cry. To top it off, the stepdaughters of the town's tourism director are hanging on their every word and action with big, worshipful eyes. Farrah's been one of the only friendly faces I've met since I got back and I don't want to jeopardize that.

Mrs. Donaldson reminded me of Molly Weasley, just a little more frazzled. She was on her way to work the evening shift at the diner out on the interstate, and clasped my hands. "They have good hearts," she reassured me before she left with a wave over her shoulder.

I don't believe her yet. I'm debating how to tactfully separate them from everyone else when I sense Mike behind me.

"How 'bout I teach them how to use a saw and a hammer?"

I close my eyes against the flutter of his breath against my nape and the way the timbre of his voice in my ear sends shivers down my spine. "That would be fantastic," I mutter.

He glides his fingers down the back of my upper arm before he steps away.

"Jack and Jerry, you're coming with me."

"But we want to stay here, Mr. Callihan," one of them protests.

"You can practice with everyone else later. Right now I need your help finishing up the sets."

The three of them are walking away when Addie St. Simon raises her hand and waves it madly in the air. "Ms. Cassidy!"

"Yes, Addie?"

"Can Abbie and I work on sets too?"

This morbid fascination with the older troublemakers could prove very dangerous for the success of the play. "No. I need the two of you here. The angel choir could use your help."

The girls have kept the toddlers occupied and escort them to the bathroom when necessary. They proudly informed me they just started babysitting and they're trying to drum up business. Learning from the Donaldson twins isn't the way to convince the town to trust them.

I clap my hands until I have everyone's attention. The chatter dies off and I can see them squirming in their seats. "We only have three weeks until the show. I'm depending on all of you to memorize your lines. If you don't have any lines, I'm depending on you to know where you're supposed to stand and help out with the singing."

Suzie Danzig raises her hand. She's Mary and I already extricated her from a mess caused by the Donaldsons tonight. When one of them pulled her ponytail she spilled Kool-Aid all over her clothes. She immediately burst into tears. "Ms. Cassidy, I've already learned all of my lines."

She's an officious little girl who reminds me of Nellie Olsen from *Little House on the Prairie.* I've never been the kind of person impressed by brown nosing, so I discourage her simpering whenever I can. "That's wonderful, Suzie, but most of your fellow actors haven't. We all need to be patient with one another."

"Yeah, brown noser," Lance West interjects.

I wag my finger in his direction. "That's enough. There'll be no name-calling here." *Even if I share the sentiment.*

"She's such a goody two shoes," he complains.

Lance is playing Joseph because his father's the preacher. I can tell he's one of those kids who resents his ties to the church and wants to walk on the wild side a little. He probably wasn't given a choice about participating and I heard him offer the Donaldson twins fifty dollars to take his place.

I know he's not happy to be here, but Joseph and Mary have to get along. The audience will be able to tell from their body language up on stage if they can't stand each other. "Suzie deserves your respect as your fellow cast member. Apologize immediately."

His expression turns mutinous.

I glare and cross my arms.

He rolls his eyes and turns toward his co-star. "Sorry, Suzie," he mumbles.

By the time practice wraps up, I feel like I've been herding cats for hours. I'm not keen to make conversation, but Farrah Caldwell pulls me aside when she picks up her stepdaughters.

"I know we haven't had the chance to talk, but I appreciate what you're doing. The girls are really excited."

"I appreciate their enthusiasm. And their help with the younger kids – they'll make great babysitters."

Farrah's face lights up and she slides her hand over the subtle curve of her stomach. "We haven't told them yet that they'll have a new family member to practice on too."

She's glowing when she makes the revelation. "Congratulations," I tell her. "When are you due?"

"I'm due in June. On our first wedding anniversary. It was a little unexpected, but we're happy."

"Well if there's anything I can do to help, let me know." I know next to nothing about kids, but I can always find something for them to do.

She laughs. "That's not what I wanted to talk to you about. I wondered if you'd be interested in joining my friends and I for our monthly movie night. Since the holiday movie marathons have started, that's how we're spending this Saturday night."

"I don't know if I can," I hedge. The more connections I make here, the harder it will be to walk away when I find my out. And I've never been good at female friendships.

Farrah lays her hand on my forearm. "Please consider it. Mike said you've been away a long time and I'm sure it's hard."

"I'll think about it."

"That's all I'll ask for now. If you decide to join us, we're congregating at Taren's. She and Zane run Hayes Orchard and Cidery and their farm is on the outskirts of town, off Brightmeadow Lane."

I wave goodbye as she walks away. Maybe I will join them. Mom has her knitting circle on Saturday evenings, and she's been nagging me to make friends.

Chapter Three

Mike

My brother is one of the most buttoned-up, holds his own counsel, people I know. But he's a great listener and when he does say something, it's on point and usually the perfect solution.

"She's back," I mumble morosely over my pizza.

It's our weekly Friday night football ritual - pizza from Salvatori's, beer and ESPN on the wide screen with surround sound. I don't know how Derek swings it, but he never has to work night shift during football season. There are only three other deputies, so the tradeoff has to be a nightmare. He's probably doing their laundry or mucking out stalls.

Or maybe he volunteers for the graveyard shift for the rest of the year. He's always stuck working Christmas and New Year's Eve, so maybe that's the sacrifice he makes.

When I don't elaborate Derek shakes his head. "There's only one girl that ever made you question the entire meaning of your life. Bianca."

"Dude. It's like she never left and time just stood still until WHAM SHAZAAM I'm in deep again the second I see her."

"Maybe you need a catharsis."

"A catharsis? You mean like an exorcism?

"No. You need to ger her out of your system for good. Maybe the only way to do that is to bang her and kill all those fantasies."

I don't think that's the answer. I think it'll just make my infatuation worse. "What if banging her has the opposite effect?"

He shrugs. "It's a chance you have to take if you ever really wanna know for sure."

I almost kissed her behind the curtains the day we were re-introduced. And I swear she has more freckles scattered across the bridge of her nose. I always wondered if she had them sprinkled in other places too. Maybe she'll let me play connect the dots or draw constellations on her skin.

"So you think I should ask her out?"

He cocks his head. "Yeah, that would be the logical place to start."

Great, my younger brother thinks I'm an idiot with no chill when it comes to women. "I have game," I defensively tell him.

His eyes glimmer with a hint of mischief. "I never said you didn't, Big Brother. But I never thought I'd see the day you came to me for advice about a woman."

"I wasn't really asking for advice."

He snorts. "If you say so. Just do me a favor and don't let on how much you like her. Or that you never stopped liking her. Letting a woman know you've carried a torch for that long makes you sound desperate."

"I've been married."

Derek rolls his eyes. "Your marriage doesn't count. It only lasted for a year. You didn't even make it out of the honeymoon stage."

"We weren't right for each other. And she was on the rebound. As soon as her ex was free again she filed for divorce. The only good thing that came out of that fiasco was the kid."

"It would have ended anyway, bro. You never got over Bianca Cassidy. And yeah, Brady definitely makes life more interesting."

"It's not like that. I was over her when I got married."

"You can lie to me, but don't lie to yourself. Tell me what your plans are this weekend." He crosses his arms and raises a brow.

"I'm fixing some fence for Bianca's mom."

"And if you catch a glimpse of your lifelong crush in the process it's a bonus."

"That's not why I'm helping out. I've been helping out for the last ten years."

"You need to examine why that is, because you're a good guy, but your motives aren't entirely pure."

He's wrong. My motives have always been pure. Serena Cassidy, Bianca's mom, always treated me like a son, and I couldn't let her farm or business suffer when Bianca abandoned her. I've been helping out for the last ten years because she's special to me in her own right. It breaks my heart that her cancer is out of remission.

"You're wrong. They've always been pure. Because I never expected her to come back."

"Well she's back now and maybe it's a good thing all around. You can finally do something about the way she's haunted your life."

"I'm gonna follow your advice and ask her out. We'll see where it goes from there."

———◆———

I knock on the back door at six a.m. She flings open the door on the second rap, her brows lowered in distress.

Bianca motions me inside and quietly shuts the door behind us. "She's having a really bad morning and finally fell asleep again."

I keep my eyes on her face instead of the long, long legs that stretch below the hem of shorts so abbreviated they should be outlawed. The ragged t-shirt she's wearing isn't much better. It has a hole in one armpit and it's falling off her shoulder. The cotton is so worn it's almost threadbare, and I swear I caught a glimpse of peaked nipple behind the fabric. She's completely unaware of the effect her sleepwear is having on my anatomy.

I clear my throat. "Is there anything I can do? I'm here to repair the fence in the west pasture."

"I could use some company over my morning coffee."

I've tried staying away because of the way she makes me feel. Tongue-tied and stumbling and on the edge of my seat. But what's the harm in a cup of coffee?

"Come in if you're going to. It's not like I'm going to lace it with arsenic or something."

She holds the screen door open, hopping from one foot to the other because it's a frosty morning.

"Coffee sounds great," I mumble as I brush past her. I sit down at the battered Formica table and pick up the newspaper.

"Do you still drink it black?"

I'm surprised she remembered. Her mom started letting us have it when we were twelve and I love the way it smells when it's undiluted by cream and sugar. "Yep. Do you still use the paper to hunt for yard sales?"

She hands me the cup she just poured and lowers herself into the seat across from me. "Yep. Best place to score vintage clothes and vinyl. I already circled a couple for next weekend."

I sip the coffee and remember the way she used to dig through the boxes from someone's garage looking for old show tune records. I'll never forget the look on her face the day she found a pristinely preserved copy of Cole Porter's *Anything Goes.* "What made you start collecting them?"

She laughs. "Mom, of course. She wore out her cast recordings of *The Sound of Music* and *My Fair Lady*. It was always my dream to strut across the stage belting out *The Rain in Spain* as Eliza Doolittle."

"Did you ever get the chance?" I'll never tell her I kept up with her career and I know the answer to the question.

"No, and it's something I still hope will happen someday."

"You could always just serenade the town after the pageant."

"*My Fair Lady* isn't a Christmas play. It wouldn't fit."

I shrug, because I don't think the audience would care. "You'd make it fit."

She shakes her head, her expression unreadable. "My voice isn't the same. I don't think it ever will be."

I'll never forget the first time I heard her sing. It was the sixth-grade talent show and she closed her eyes, clasped her hands and broke into *My Favorite Things*. She'd been humming it for a week, but whenever I asked why, she changed the subject. When her voice soared over me I was hurt because I'd never heard anything so beautiful and I couldn't believe she hadn't shared it with me. Later on, I realized I fell in love with her that day, while she was standing in a pool of light holding an entire audience captive. I'd probably loved her since the day she peeked her head over the fence that separated our yards and blasted me with her water gun. But that's the first time I couldn't imagine my life without her.

Singing was everything to her, and my heart breaks at her confession. "Just because it's changed doesn't mean it's different in a bad way. I bet you still sound like an angel."

She snorts. "An angel who smokes three packs a day. It's raspy now, and I can't hit the higher registers."

"But you just need to rest and it'll come back, right?" I can see the shattered pieces of her dream laying at her feet. Even though I want her to stay here, I don't want that mess to be the cost.

"I don't know."

She sounds defeated and I need to distract her. "Are you sure there's nothing you need me to fix besides the fence line?"

"I've been meaning to check the propane level in the tank outside. Mom can't remember when she filled it up."

"Done. Are you sure there's nothing else?" I want to ask if she'll let me fix her.

"No."

I get up and make it to the door before her hand lands on my forearm. I can feel her touch even through my fleece-lined flannel. "Yeah?" I clear my throat and ask.

"Thanks, Callihan. For everything. I appreciate the way you've taken care of her and the farm and the store. I know it wasn't easy and I want you to know I'm grateful."

"I didn't do it so I could hold it over your head."

"I know. You did it because that's who you are. The guy who takes care of people."

"I would have taken care of you too if you'd let me." I want to take back the raw confession as soon as it leaves my mouth.

"I know that too." She removes her hand, her expression inscrutable. "Be careful out there and make sure you come in for lunch if you're still here. I'm making Mom's cheesy potato soup."

"I will," I reassure her without looking back. And then I hightail it out of there before I lose the last shred of my dignity and beg her to stay in Willow Creek so I can show her how well I'll take care of her.

Chapter Four

Bianca

Farrah's friends are all laid back and happily in love. Not the least bit catty. They could easily become my inner circle.

"I have a Bianca Cassidy playlist in my streaming account," Taren tells me.

"I think those days might be behind me," I confess. "I don't think the vocal surgery worked."

Emma and Sarah's eyes darken in sympathy and all four of them gasp.

"That's a tragedy."

Sarah's observation is like the twist of a blade between my ribs. "I hope all I need to do is rest my voice and do the exercises my therapist insisted on."

Emma cocks her head to the side. "What'll you do if a return to Broadway isn't in the cards?"

"I guess I'll have to figure something out."

"There's always the feed store. It's the only one in town and some of the guys your Mom hires are disrespectful idiots."

"I think Mike Callihan has been helping her run it."

Farrah glowers. "Then I'm going to have a word with him about the way some of them talk about my sister. I'm surprised River hasn't already taken care of it."

Taren raises a brow. "I know you're protective since the two of you made up, but how do you know River hasn't already taken care of it?"

"I feel like I'm missing essential intel," I say as my gaze flashes back and forth between the two of them.

Sarah draws me close so she whisper in my ear. "Farrah's talking about her half-sister Roxie. She's with River. He used to be her farmhand and he's a lot younger. But he worships the ground she walks on. Even though he's a golden retriever, I'm pretty sure he'd pulverize anyone he heard talking smack."

"Willow Creek seems to have a lot of recent happily ever afters."

Emma must have a sarcasm detector, because she's the one that laughs. "I didn't believe in them either. But Willow Creek has a way of making lemonade out of the lemons in your life."

"I have a lot of lemons, and I think Mike Callihan might be one of them," I say as I tip back my glass of wine.

Taren leans forward, her chin in her hand. "Maybe he's a lemon meringue – those are a lot easier to accept."

"Once upon a time I thought he was."

Now Farrah leans forward. "So you two have a history?"

I gulp the rest of the wine and push my hair behind my ears. "Ancient history."

"Okay, now you have to tell us the whole story," Emma demands.

Sarah gives me a troubled look and I think she senses how uneasy I am with the direction of the conversation. "Maybe it's not something she wants to talk about."

I toss her a grateful smile. "Sarah's right. I'm not ready to talk about him yet. I didn't even know he stayed in Willow Creek."

Taren sighs dreamily. "I'm a sucker for a second chance romance."

"They hardly ever work," mutters Sarah.

"You and Zane just got lucky," Farrah says.

Taren raises a brow. "Why are all of you such skeptics?"

"They're not skeptics. It's usually true. Most of the time whatever heartache caused the breakup is too defining to sweep under the rug."

Taren tilts her head and studies me. "So you had a defining heartache with Mike Callihan?"

"Not really, but I think I may have been his."

"Oof," Emma exhales. "Guys usually hold grudges longer than women. I don't think there are going to be any make out sessions behind the curtains."

Farrah snorts. "I wouldn't be so sure. You should see the way he stares at her when her back is turned. Like a hungry puppy."

A hungry puppy? I don't know why the thought of him pining turns my bones to mush. And I can't use wine to brush it aside because my glass is empty.

I reluctantly rise to my feet. "I think I should call it a night. I have errands to run in the morning." Tomorrow is Mom's last bout of treatment for the week.

Farrah, Emma and Sarah all rise as well.

Taren jumps up and gives each of us a hug. Even me.

"Let's do this again soon. Maybe after bookclub this month?"

"Bookclub?" I was in one with a bunch of my fellow actors in the city and I miss the discussion and the camaraderie.

"Yeah, bookclub. You have to come to the next meeting." Taren insists.

"What do you guys read?"

"I never thought I'd be a fan of historical romance, but it's my jam now." Emma chimes in. "We're working our way through Julie Anne Long's *Palace of Rogue* series right now."

"Do I have to read them in order?" I don't know of I'll have the time to catch up to wherever they are.

Sarah shakes her head. "Nope. We're reading the third one right now, *I'm Only Wicked With You*. The hero, Hugh, is a lumbersnack. You'll love it."

"Is there an audio version available?" That way I can listen while I do farm and house chores.

"That's how I usually finish the books. The librarian, Ms. Bromwell, always makes sure the audiobook is available in the catalog."

"Since the audio is available, I'll try to make time to join you." I thread my arms through the sleeves of my jacket and wind my scarf around my neck.

"There's something I want to talk to you about. Can you meet me for coffee in the morning at Cupcake on Main? Around nine?"

"Can we make it ten thirty? I have to take Mom to her appointment at eight."

Her eyes fill with sympathy. "Of course. I'll see you then."

I'm sitting at one of the outdoor tables, nursing the cinnamon roll iced latte Emma suggested, when Farrah takes the seat across from me.

"Good morning," I say. It is a good morning for the most part. The air is crisp since it's mid -November, but I can still feel the sun on my face. And Mom's treatment went well this morning. I left her bundled on the couch and asked Mike's mom to check on her around noon.

"Good morning."

"You're very chirpy for a Monday morning."

She laughs and it's like a sprinkle of powdered sugar. "I don't mind Mondays because I love my job."

"Is your job the reason for this coffee date? Mike told me you and the mayor have grand schemes."

She sets her coffee on a napkin and rests her chin in her hands. Her gaze is filled with excitement. "I don't know how long you're staying, or if you'd be interested, but they finally settled the estate for the old Majestic Theatre."

I wrinkle my brow. "Why do we need to discuss that?"

"Well, the town might be buying it to create a cultural arts hub. The mayor and I were talking yesterday about making it the home of community theatre productions."

"We had our sixth-grade talent show there. I remember the acoustics are fabulous. It was shabby even then. It's been closed for so long, I bet it's pretty dilapidated."

"If we can convince the town council it's a solid investment, we could really use someone with your experience and connections to lead it."

I laugh self-consciously. "I'm used to the spotlight, not the behind-the-scenes stuff. I'd probably make a hash of it."

"Don't sell yourself short," Farrah admonished. "I think you'd be great. And sometimes it's good to have someone at the helm with a fresh perspective. Can I give your contact info to the realtor, Cindy Davis? I think you know her. She went to Willow Creek with you and Mike. She was the head cheerleader."

So his prom date never left Willow Creek. I wonder if they had a fling after I left. "Sure. Why do you need me to speak with her?"

"Before we pitch this idea in front of the council, we need a realistic idea of how much work would need to be done to restore it. Since you've been in theatre your whole life, we thought your insight would really help."

"I can help with that, but I don't know much about building integrity or stuff like that."

She grabs my hand across the table. "Thank you so much! I know the more stuff like this we do, the greater the appeal for families with young children to move here. If we build a rich, interactive cultural arts scene, it'll help lure them away from the city. And

we're going to have Mike inspect the building for structural issues."

Chapter Five

Mike

I HAND OVER AN iced maple latte from Cupcake on Main and drop into the seat next to her. She has a pile of paperwork in her lap, but she's staring at the raised dais with a bemused look on her face.

"Zane said you're thinking about running the Majestic." I don't say I hope the rumors are true. If she's considering it, that means she's considering other stuff too. Like staying here for good.

She snorts. "So the town gossip mill is still going strong. Farrah just told me about it over lunch. I haven't had time to think about anything. Are you trying to bribe me with this latte?"

"I never said I wouldn't resort to bribery if it'll convince you to stay. So you're thinking about it?" I hold my breath and wait for her answer.

"I don't know, Callihan. Maybe. I always thought I'd never come back here. And running a community theater is a lot of work. Probably way more work than doing a Broadway show because usually there aren't deep pockets to keep everything from going off the rails. I don't know if I want to get stuck herding cats on a shoestring budget."

"Can it really be that bad?"

"Yep. I have friends all over the country who do it and they swear it's all held together with duct tape and dental floss."

"Isn't there grant money available to fill in the gaps?"

Her laugh is sarcastic this time. "Art programs and initiatives everywhere have been gutted in favor of math and science. I don't know if I have the strength to fight those battles."

"The town could really use a creative outlet like this. Farrah and Zane asked me to inspect it. If the town decides to buy it, I could help you fix it up. That place is the biggest eyesore on Main Street and the consensus down at Curl Up and Dye is that you're the perfect candidate to breathe life back into it."

"So the salon is still a hotbed of conspiracy and speculation."

"At least they're excited about the possibility and don't think it's a waste of time or money."

She takes a sip of the latte and leans back. "At least there's that."

Her admission is wry, and I wonder how hard the town has been on her since she returned. "They didn't exactly roll out the red carpet for you."

"Nope," she confesses in the middle of another sip. "I think a lot of them see this pageant as nothing more than a break from their kids in the evening. Most of the parents don't stay for practice and I had to beg my friends in the city for costumes since no one in Willow Creek seemed willing to volunteer their time or sewing skills. At least Farrah invited me to girls' night. Which was amazing."

"It's the first pageant since we were kids. Just give them the chance to warm up to the idea. And I'm friends with all of the other halves you partied with, so I know you were in good hands."

"I don't think people warming up to the idea is the problem, Callihan. I think too much has changed and the things we grew up with just aren't a priority. Farrah and her friends were encouraging, but I didn't expect everything to be this hard."

"Well Zane and Farrah are on a mission to restore a sense of community and this pageant is a way to bring everyone together for the holidays."

"I haven't met the mayor yet, but Farrah is one of the most relentlessly determined people I've ever met. I can see why he made her the town's marketing and tourism director."

Farrah is relentless. Probably because her twin stepdaughters keep her on her toes. She's probably in permanent manic mode to keep up with them. "She is. She even convinced her husband to start a local star-gazing academy about twenty miles out of town. It's an abandoned farm Blake Armitage snapped up because it was adjacent to his equine therapy facility. He donated it to the town's rec department. She said we can bill it as a dark sky space."

"Aren't most of those out west?"

"Yeah, but she thinks all the commuters in the DC area will flock here because it's a quick jaunt. They'll be able to commune with nature and stop at Wegner's on the way home."

"If she has all of that planned, why is she so adamant about the Majestic? There are plenty of other tourism magnets."

"Maybe. But the Majestic could be a way to lure people who want to relocate, not just tourists."

"Won't it create more work for you? You seem to have your hands full as the Public Works Director. I see you as often as I see your employees."

I casually slide my arm behind her chair. "You know I was never the sit behind a desk type, Cassidy. My new project could be helping you fix up the Majestic."

She gives me a quizzical look. "I thought the last thing you wanted was to be near me."

I shrug, suddenly uncomfortable. She's right. But not for the reasons she thinks. "It's for the betterment of the town. Kind of part of my job description."

"Well I thought the town was going to hire a contractor, but if I decide to take on the renovation and you want to help instead of enjoying your downtime, it would mean more money for the other stuff we need, like costumes and props and new lighting."

"If that means you'll be here longer, I'm in. My job's usually only nine to five. We could work on it together in the evenings and on weekends." I volunteer, even as I question why I'm walking toward the guillotine like I don't care about the wicked blade that's going to make my head roll.

"I'm not making any promises, Callihan. That isn't what this is about. I just figured I'm here, and I don't know what my future looks like and it's time to give back to the community that's been a safety net for Mom since I left."

"I'll take what I can get, Cassidy." I reach for her hand and when I link our pinky fingers like I did when we were ten and holding the line during Red Rover at recess, she doesn't pull away. I don't care if I sound needy or unhinged because she's all I've ever wanted.

"I'm still pretty determined to leave, Callihan."

I flash a grin in her direction. "Pretty deter-mined is a long way from gung ho. I think I'm weakening your resolve."

She just shakes her head and laughs.

Chapter Six

Bianca

The realtor called me yesterday and asked if I wanted to tour the theater this morning. I don't know why I said yes, because I still haven't decided whether or not I'm going to stay. I was up half the night hemming the robes for the angel choir, and if I stay here and resurrect the community playhouse that's what my life will consist of.

I'm barreling around the corner of the stairs when I collide with something solid. Strong arms surround me as I upend my hot coffee. I can feel the fiery liquid and his heat seeping through my shirt, and somehow I lost one of my ballet flats when I tumbled forward. "Ouch," I mumble.

His face is suddenly right there and I should be hoping I'm not going to have red boobs from coffee burn or somehow wedge a splinter into my bare foot. Instead, I'm holding my breath and waiting for him to finally press those chiseled lips to mine. So I can compare the way they feel now to the way they felt then. Because they're right there.

"What were you running from, Bumble Bee?"

It's the first time since we were eighteen that he's used the nickname he gave me. The rasp of his gruff voice hits me in the solar plexus and sends tingles up my spine. I'm pretty sure he's using it to force me into remembering where we've been and what we were. What could have been if I'd stayed.

I try to lean away, but his grip is too firm. "Just now, I wasn't running from anything." I'm going to assume he was talking about the here and now, because I'm not going to revisit my reasons for running nineteen years ago. I hope he doesn't press me for a deeper explanation, because it's already hard to maintain my dignity when I'm balanced on one leg and clutching his upper arms for dear life.

He shakes his head and gives me a bemused smile. "Always cryptic and making me work for answers. If you weren't running from something, what were you running to?"

"I have a meeting with the realtor this morning about the Majestic." I brace myself for his reaction.

His eyes gleam down at me and I almost get lost in the sparks of gold nestled in the muddy brown depths. "Which realtor?"

"Your old flame, Cindy Houlihan. Except now she's Cindy Davis."

I expect him to jump on my words.

"Do you want company? I'd like to get a better look at some of the plumbing and electrical. And I didn't have time last week to examine the floors."

I should tell him no because when he's near my decision-making ability is severely impaired. I should tell him no because he's the reason I was distracted and tripped and spilled my coffee. Because he filled my thoughts so much I couldn't sleep and ended up hemming robes until two o'clock in the morning. I should tell him no because he's the reason I'll probably get tetanus from stepping on a nail before I can find my shoe.

I'm weak – because I don't tell him no. "Sure, if you think you won't get bored."

His warm chuckle floats between us and there goes another hit to my chest.

"One thing you'll never do is bore me, Cassidy."

He shifts me to the side so I'm leaning against the wall and I already miss his touch and the way his voice scratched when he used my old nickname.

"Hold onto the wall and let me find your shoe. You don't need a splinter or god forbid, tetanus. Once I find your shoe, I'm grabbing you the hoodie I have stashed in the truck so you can change out of your wet sweater."

He's taking care of me just like he always did. And the way he read my mind just proves he can still see the wheels turning in my head. If I'm not careful, he's going to figure out he's the only one who can convince me to stay in Willow Creek.

When he comes back down the stairs, he's holding a faded Hokies hoodie and my lost shoe. He kneels in front of me and lifts my foot to his thigh. He circles my ankle when he slips my shoe on and it makes my knees weak.

He stands again and tosses me the hoodie. "Strip and put this on. I'll turn around so you can protect your delicate sensibilities."

He crosses his arms and gives me his back. When I slip the hoodie over my head, I'm surrounded by the scent of cedar sawdust and lemon. I bury my head in the collar and inhale. It's warm and comfy because the fleece is washed-too-many-times soft against my skin.

"Thanks, this is much warmer."

He turns back around and his eyes darken. "I like seeing you in my clothes, Cassidy."

I gulp. "Don't read more into this than spilled coffee, Callihan," I say to cover my confusion.

"I know better than that. You've made it pretty clear your non-negotiable agenda has a begin and end date. I'm not trying to convince you, just stating a fact - *I like seeing you in my clothes.*"

I wonder what one of his worn t-shirts would feel like and if it'd brush the tops of my thighs or hang to my knees.

"Well, thanks again for the save, regardless of whether you had an ulterior motive."

"No ulterior motive. Because I didn't expect to like it as much as I do. But I should have known."

He mutters the last two sentences under his breath, like he's afraid to voice them out loud.

"Come on." He grabs my hand. "Since you're letting me tag along we're taking my truck instead of the tin can your mom calls a car."

I love driving my mom's candy apple red Mini Cooper, but he would look like a gorilla smashed into one of those tiny little dune buggies. "Fine. Can I replace my coffee on the way?"

"Yeah, I need a refill too."

By the time we stroll into Cupcake on Main, the morning rush is over. Emma gives me a knowing look when we get to the counter.

"Hey Mike, are you having your usual?" She asks him.

"Yeah, gimme an Americano. And whatever Bumble Bee wants."

Emma raises a brow and smirks. "What'll you have, Bumble Bee?"

I give her the evil eye I to let her know it is never okay to call me that. "I'll take the Hazelnut Mocha on ice."

Mike hands her a twenty before I can protest. "I've got this. Don't argue," he tells me when he sees my facial expression.

"Your bumble bee is slowly making her way through the entire fall drink menu."

"So you take your coffee with more than half and half now?"

I shrug. "When it's available."

Cindy is waiting outside the theater when we park at the meter. She waves her hand excitedly and I wonder if she's going to revisit her head cheerleader days and jump up and down.

"Let's go inside. I can't wait to show you the potential. It just needs a little elbow grease and it can be the star of Main Street again."

When a realtor from one of the boroughs tells you something needs a little elbow grease it usually means it's barely salvageable and they're desperate.

When she opens the door and flicks the switch, nothing happens. Mike and I exchange a look because this doesn't bode well for "the potential."

"No worries. I always carry a flashlight in my purse." She hauls out a high beam like the one exterminators use to crawl under houses. It's huge. And very, very bright.

The first thing I notice is the chairs. They all need reupholstering. The vintage red velvet is faded and full of tiny moth holes.

The second thing I notice is the floor. It's sloping on one side.

"Rotten boards, maybe the joist too," Mike mutters.

"The heirs have been fighting over the estate for eighteen years, and it's sat here empty that whole time." It looks like it's been empty for much longer than that.

"Do you think it's salvageable?" I whisper from the corner of my mouth.

He nods. "Definitely."

I motion Cindy over. "Hey Cindy. I think we have all the information we need. I'm going to speak with Farrah and Zane."

She takes my hand when I offer it, her eyes glowing. "Thank you, Bianca. I want you to know how excited my girls and I are that you're here. We saw you in *Rent* and we've been starstruck ever since."

Well, that's a development I never expected. I was way beneath Cindy Houlihan's radar in high school. "Thanks, Cindy. I'm very grateful for all the opportunities I've had."

She hasn't stopped smiling. "I'm so honored to have renewed our acquaintance. I hope you decide to settle here again. Your star power would really help Willow Creek."

Once we're standing on the sidewalk again, Mike throws his arm over my shoulders.

The weight, both unfamiliar and familiar at the same time, makes my nape prickle. It feels companionable and proprietary. I wonder if Cindy Houlihan Davis is watching us.

"So, Cassidy, how's a waffle cone sound?"

"Mike, what person in their right mind has ice cream for lunch in the middle of November?" It used to be one of our Sunday rituals. Rain or shine. Sleet or snow. Kind of like things that aren't supposed to prevent the mail delivery. But it was just for kicks because we were kids and had a lot of energy and were never cold. My adult internal barometer isn't exactly compatible with ice cream in late fall.

"Us persons."

His loaded answer takes me back to a day I'll never forget and I swallow. "Sure."

⸺◈⸺

The Dairy Freeze hasn't changed in the twenty years since I left and I bet the plastic menu with the red retro type nailed to the side of the building has been there since my mom was a kid.

The only difference is who waited on us. Mabel Sinclair was like a grouchy cafeteria lunch lady. Her granddaughter, Jenny Sinclair runs it now. Her eyes widened when we walked up to the take-out window.

"Oh my gosh. You're Bianca Cassidy," she'd breathlessly said.

"Yep, that's me," I'd replied.

She fumbled the order a little bit, and Mike whispered. "Another starstruck fan."

We ordered the same thing we used to order when we were sixteen. Vanilla for him and chocolate with sprinkles for me.

"So, a taste of yours for a taste of mine?"

When he leans in, I want to meet him halfway. I thrust my ice cream cone in front of me instead and offer it to him. "Sure."

I watch his tongue lap up a rivulet of chocolate, and a bright blue sprinkle gets caught in his mustache.

I want to climb onto the table, crawl forward and lick it off.

Even though his vanilla cone is dripping onto my mittens and over his hands, I can't look away.

When he licks his lips, I copy him, and catch a drop of the vanilla bean infused soft serve sliding down the side of his cone.

I can't believe the Dairy Freeze is still open year-round, and even though this isn't technically a date, it feels like one. Trading tastes of our waffle cones at one of the weathered gray picnic tables is just like it used to be.

We're so much more now than we were when we did this as smitten teenagers who refused to admit the way we felt. I watch him and it doesn't matter how much we were then or how we came back to this déjà vu moment that's like a hook in my chest.

I feel the same way I did that day – when I finally realized Mike Callihan hung the sun and moon. Breathless anticipation. Smoldering eyes underneath those sooty lashes that make me blush. The tingle that starts in my toes and settles just behind my lips.

"You're looking at me like you want to kiss me, Cassidy," he says as he grins.

"That's how you're looking at me too," I tell him and give into temptation. I lean in and brush the sprinkle from his mustache with my tongue.

When I go to sit back down, he clasps my upper arms. "Not yet," he murmurs. "Turnabout is fair play."

And then his lips feather over my cheeks and kiss the corners of my mouth. That's all he does. I want to feel the full press of his lips on mine, but he's not going to oblige me today.

"You had a speck of ice cream too," he explains.

I raise a skeptical brow. "On my cheeks? I don't think I believe you, Callihan."

He shrugs. "Since you don't have your compact handy, you'll just have to take my word for it."

———◦———

That evening when Farrah picks up the twins, she pulls me aside. "My friend Mari told me she saw you and Callihan kissing at the Dairy Freeze this afternoon."

"We weren't kissing. Not exactly. When we were kids, we used to go there every Sunday and trade bites of each other's cones."

She gives me a mischievous smile. "Sounds like a ritual to me."

"Just a moment of nostalgia. Nothing more."

"If you say so. At least tell me how you ended up at the Dairy Freeze."

"Cindy Houlihan wanted me to look at the Majestic and he tagged along."

She squeals. "Yay! Does this mean you're staying?"

"I haven't made up my mind yet. The theater needs a ton of work. Mike thinks it'll need something pretty close to a ground up restoration."

Her expression sobers. "That's what I told Zane, so I'm glad the two of you are corroborating it. I'm going to start looking for some grants that can cover the acquisition and the restoration. Let me know if there are any you think we're eligible for."

"That's not really my realm of expertise, but I have friends I can reach out to." I need to catch up with Cheryl, anyway. She left Broadway seven years ago to go back to northwestern Ohio and care for her parents. She's been waist deep in the community theater there ever since.

Chapter Seven

Mike

Thanksgiving weekend is almost here, and mom told me to invite Bianca and Serena. I lingered after rehearsal tonight in the hope of getting her alone so I could ask. Evidently Cindy has been talking, because all of the moms showed up tonight, and some of the dads, when they picked up the kids. Like now they know exactly who Bianca is, they think it's a legitimate endeavor or she's lending it credibility. It pisses me off that they are so small-minded. I love Willow Creek, but it's easy to forget how self-absorbed some community members can become. They'll stay away and let everyone else do the grunt work until they think they have the chance to soak up some glory or brush their wings with someone notorious. I'm painting the main backdrop to look like a picture I once saw of Mt. Sinai, when I hear her footsteps come to a halt behind me.

"You're really good at this."

She sounds amazed by my competency, and I should be offended by her lack of trust. Instead, I blush. I never blush.

I hitch my left shoulder to my ear as I shrug and keep my face turned away so she won't see how red my cheeks are underneath my beard. "That's because I've done it before. I like painting murals. I was thinking of that old gospel song, Go Tell it on the Mountain."

"You're full of secrets, Callihan. Since when do you paint murals? Anything here in town?"

I focus on the getting the color of the sky just right so I won't have to look at her when I answer. "The old O'Brien place."

I heard the catch in her breath and I bet her eyes snapped wide open. "The haunted house?" She asks in disbelief.

"It wasn't haunted," I tell her. "Just neglected. You should see it now."

"Who owns it? Do you think they'd take me on a tour?"

I know if I touched her right now she'd be quivering with excitement.

"I own it. And yes I'll give you a tour."

"That's a big house for a bachelor."

There's a question buried somewhere in that observation. "Yeah. But I wasn't a bachelor when I bought it."

"You're married?"

"Not anymore." It didn't feel like I was married even when I was married, because Carrie would never be Bianca. We tried, and I loved her with the tiny part of my heart that didn't belong to the girl who left, but it wasn't enough. And she hated small town life. "My wife asked for a dissolution a year after our son was born."

"You have a son. Somehow, I never imagined that."

She sounds wistful.

"Carrie and I co-parent Brady. She probably resents the fact that she can't move closer to the city, but there was no way I wasn't going to be a part of Brady's life."

"How old is he?" She kneels beside me and grabs a brush. Her shoulder bumps mine as she starts swiping green paint along the bottom of the panel.

"He's eight. And you never told me you were a painter too."

She shrugs and flushes just like I did a minute ago. "I dabble in watercolors, and everyone who does theater has to kind of become a jill of all trades. But I'm just the pinch hitter, and there's always the possibility I'll strike out. I'm nothing even close to a master. Not like you."

"I'm not a master either, but sometimes it's a great outlet for the way I feel when I can't put things in a box or ignore them."

She smiles wistfully. "That sounds like it could be really useful sometimes."

"I could cook dinner for us if you want to take a tour of the house tomorrow night."

When she turns around, the paintbrush is dangling from her hand and she's grinning. "Are you officially asking me out, Callihan?"

Suddenly my face is burning again. I'm supposed to be asking her to Thanksgiving dinner next week, not my house. But if she says yes, I can ask her the other question then. I shrug. "If that's the label you wanna give it."

She tips her head to the side. "What other label is there?"

"Just a couple of old friends catching up."

"You can call it that if you want. But I'm still going to call it a date. Especially if Farrah hears about it. Maybe she'll get off my case then."

"Why's Farrah on your case?"

"Our visit to Dairy Freeze was heartily observed and well-documented."

"You can use me as prop, Cassidy. I don't mind."

"I don't consider you a prop, Callihan. If I tell her we're going on a date, she'll stop trying to think of ways to throw us together."

"I'm glad to be of assistance. You can bring the wine."

"Text me the directions and I'll be there at six thirty sharp."

"Dinner will be ready. Just be careful – there are a lot of deer out that way this time of year."

"I promise I'll be careful."

———— ◦○◦ ————

I want to show the house in the best light possible, so I putter around all day Saturday. I have my mom's chicken cacciatore recipe in the crockpot and the garlic bread is ready to pop in the oven. One of the Mantovani records I borrowed from my mom is in the record player. I just need to finish nailing down the loose boards in the hallway and painting over the dark spots in the oyster plaster.

I have time to do that and hop in the shower, because Bianca was always late for everything when we were growing up. I set the alarm on my phone and get to work.

Chapter Eight

Bianca

WHEN TAREN FOUND OUT I loved to thrift she told me about an estate sale happening on the edge of town today. It's on the way to the O'Brien place, so I decide to stop on my way to dinner. I'll be a little early, but I don't think my date will mind.

The house is huge. It's a late nineteenth-century farmhouse with at least five bedrooms, and every single one is filled to the brim with antiques. There are so many things I want to take home with me, but I don't have the space.

My hand glides over the top of a cherry wood piano. I started taking lessons when I was five, but it's been years since I had the time to sit on a bench. Unable to resist, I lift the lid and sit down. I glide my fingers over the keys and close my eyes. Suddenly I'm playing *Someone to Watch Over Me.*

As the last note dies, I'm surrounded by clapping. When I open my eyes, the intimate parlor is filled with an audience drawn by my impromptu concert.

I stand and bow with a smile on my face, a little embarrassed I got so carried away.

The woman who introduced herself as the executor steps forward. "Dear, I have all of your records, but I had no idea you played as well as you sing."

"You're very kind. I haven't played in a very long time. Thank you for allowing me to take advantage of your gorgeous instrument."

"It was truly a joy. It's for sale, just like everything else in the house. It should go home with someone who truly appreciates it."

"I do appreciate it, but I don't have the space for it," I regretfully tell her.

"I'll hold it for you just in case you change your mind."

"Thank you." I'm not going to change my mind. I really don't have anywhere to put it.

Here in Willow Creek or at my apartment in the city.

I buy some Cole Porter records and a chic vintage wool swing coat and head to the O'Brien farm for my date.

Everything about the farm looks different. The barn's been restored, the oaks lining the driveway have been pruned into some semblance of uniformity, and the front porch has been recently painted. The soft white paint glows under the rays of the setting sun, and as I park I notice the swing hanging in the far corner.

I knock on the door, and there's no response. I hear music, so I assume he's there. I let myself in.

I follow the trail of notes and find him crouched in front of the wainscot in the hallway.

"I'm disappointed a butler didn't greet me," I tell him.

He whirls around, startled. When he recognizes me, he grins and rises to his feet.

He's not the boy I knew and I can't help wondering if his lips are still like pillows and steel. I can't help wondering if his kiss still tastes like the cinnamon flavored toothpicks he always had hanging from the corner of his mouth.

When he crowded me against the scaffolding and braced his arms over my head, I wanted to close my eyes. I could almost feel the scratchy straw of the hay bale against my back, the trickle of sweat that pooled at my nape, and the ghost of that long ago kiss haunting the sliver of space between our bodies.

He's streaked with paint and sweat. He has a bandsaw in one hand and a hammer in the other one.

I want to tackle him to the floor.

He's even sexier now than he was twenty years ago, because all that rugged confidence is warranted. If we were stranded on a desert island he'd hack down trees, build us a shelter and then catch me dinner with his bare hands.

He'll have my back and protect me unto death when the zombie apocalypse comes.

The guys I dated in the city are nothing like him. They were polished suits and five-hundred-dollar bottles of champagne and I bought you a tennis bracelet. He's an old t-shirt and battered Levis so worn they're molded to the thighs I can't stop looking at like a second skin. He's I'll catch you when you fall and I know how you like your coffee and I remember every word you've ever said.

He's *I've known you were mine since we were fifteen and I've waited long enough for you to realize it too.*

"You're early. I wasn't expecting that."

I lift my right shoulder. "I didn't think you'd mind."

"I don't."

He doesn't drop the tools, he carefully lays them on a folding chair. He stalks toward me and I know it's a date beyond the shadow of a doubt and he's going to kiss me.

And before I can take another breath, he's on me. This kiss is hotter and sweeter than the one he gave me when we were eighteen. This kiss is like the edge of a blade or the white-hot flames that can burn everything to ash in seconds. Dangerous. So dangerous.

He scoops his hands beneath me and my legs slip around his waist as he backs me into the wall.

I can't believe he still smells the same. Like lemonade stands in the summer and a fresh cut field in the spring. Like the farm I grew up on. Like home.

He dips his head and scrapes my throat with the edge of his teeth and murmurs, "So fucking sweet."

He nips the tendon and then laves it with his tongue and wedges himself against me.

I can feel the long, hard, thick ridge of his cock through the seam of my threadbare yoga pants. I want to pull him out and revel in the way he thrusts against me because he's undone.

"So fucking perfect," I murmur back. "The way you feel."

"You took the words outta my mouth, Bumble Bee."

"Are we going to hump against a wall, Callihan?"

"We just might, Cassidy. Especially since I've been dreaming about sinking into you since 2002."

"You had dirty dreams about me when you were sixteen?"

He kisses the hollow of my throat, the softness of his beard tickling my collarbones. "Since the day we traded ice cream."

"But, what about..."

He silences me with the blunt press of his lips against mine. Hard and quick. "No more questions, Bumble Bee," he admonishes as he slides his hand underneath the hem of my shirt.

I arch back into the wall when his callused thumb grazes me over the cotton of my bra.

"Fuck, I want to see what color your nipples are," he rasps into the curve behind my ear and grazes the other one.

"What's stopping you?" I taunt. This is going way too fast and spiraling out of control and I should reel us back from the edge, but the words get stuck in my throat. Maybe this is exactly what I need. It's only our second kiss and we haven't let go since we were eighteen. But I don't care. No matter where this goes, it feels more right than anything else in my life.

"Nothing now," he growls and yanks my shirt up. He doesn't bother unhooking my bra, he just tugs the cups down.

I love how impatient he's being. Like he can't get enough of me fast enough.

He stares so long at the skin he just bared, I try to wrestle my wrists free so I can cover up.

"Nope. You're not going anywhere."

He brushes his thumb over me again, his face full of wonder and obsession. His touch is so gentle and worshipful, I close my eyes.

"I knew they'd be the same color as your lips, like little red raspberries winking up at me in the sunlight."

"I never took you for a poet, Callihan. And raspberries, really? You used to throw the rotten ones at me when we were kids."

"Yep. Even then I thought you were cute when you were mad."

I thump him in the shoulder with my fist. "So you've always had intentions."

"Just like the ones I have now – but they're all grown up and we're playing a different version of tag you're it. No more questions. Don't make me tell you again."

The way he rumbles out the warning makes my heart skip a beat, my pulse pound, and heat pool low in my stomach. Part of me wants to keep asking questions so I can find out what happens if he has to tell me again.

When his lips land on mine this time, I can see every single one of his intentions shimmering between us. When the swooping kiss becomes the slide of his thumbs over the peaks of my breasts, I squirm. He chuckles darkly and flattens me against the wall, so there's no space between our bodies and I can feel exactly how much he wants me.

He kisses the corner of my mouth again and then his lips skate down my throat and land on my breast. He sucks me into the hot vortex of his mouth, and I know his teeth and tongue will paint my nipple dark red. His hand slides under the waistband of my pants, and then he pulls them down with a determined grip.

I catch my breath when he crouches in front of me.

"I bet you wore these pretty black panties for me, Bumble Bee." His tongue strokes me through the thick silk and I moan, blindly grabbing for something to anchor me. My hands land on his ears and he laughs. "So you want to steer. I'll let you."

He dips his head again, and holy saints, how was his ex-wife able to leave him behind if he's so good at this? I'm glad she's an idiot.

I tug on his hair. "Come back up here for a second."

He blinks up at me like I lost my mind. "No woman has ever said that to me while I'm doing this," he smirks.

"Do you think we're moving too fast?" I could kick the voice of my conscience or whatever it is, but I need to make sure this is what I want and need. This is more than a flare of heat we can't ignore. This is something that's been building our whole lives and I don't want to ruin everything.

He rises to his feet and drops his forehead to mine. "I don't think so. I've been waiting for you for most of my life, Bumble Bee." He takes a deep breath and I feel the vibration where his chest is pressed against mine. "But if you're having second thoughts about me and what's happening, tell me now. Because I can wait as long as I need to and I don't want to mess this up."

His deep brown gaze is earnest and I can see the way he feels about me flickering in its depths.

"I'm not going to let us mess this up," I tell him.

"I won't either. Now," he starts sliding back down my body. "Can I pick up where I left off?"

All I can manage is a grunt of assent when I feel the tickle of his beard against my inner thigh. He slides his nose down the crease, skating it along the elastic of my bikini briefs. He sets his mouth against my center and blows against the damp fabric, and then he slips his thumb and forefinger under the edge. He flicks his thumb over my clit and sinks his finger in just past the first knuckle.

"Don't let the dinner burn."

"Nothing's going to burn except you, Cassidy. I already turned down the crock-pot and there's nothing that needs my attention right now besides you."

"How long have you been prepping for my arrival?"

He looks up at me through his long dark lashes. "I thought I said no more questions."

"You know I ask questions when I get nervous."

"You have no reason to be nervous, sweetheart. It's just us. Mike and Bianca. I'll take care of you."

I've never been able to let go with someone. The only way I've ever been able to come is with a vibrator and my imagination. I decide it'd probably be a good idea to manage his expectations. "Guys aren't usually able to do that with me, so consider yourself warned. I don't want your ego bruised when this doesn't end with me screaming your name."

"Well, I'm going to take my time and make sure that's not the case. Pretty sure my ego will remain intact."

He starts exploring again, and the feel of his breath right there, and the stroke of his thumb and the thrust of his finger, like he has all the time in the world and I was made to worship, starts getting to me.

When I roll my hips to chase his caress, his laughter rumbles against me. "Told you," he murmurs.

He finally tugs my underwear aside and replaces his thumb with his tongue. He sucks me into his mouth, and my clit throbs when he glides the edge of his teeth over it. "Oh my god," I moan.

"I thought you said you wouldn't be screaming my name."

I should correct him. But I don't. Because he must be a god to make me feel this way. Or maybe it's because we have this history and he's been watching me and wanting this our whole lives. He knows exactly how to push me over the edge.

When he thrusts his finger into my channel again, the leg I didn't even realize I threw over his shoulder starts to quiver. I shatter and my head thuds against the wall. "Holy shit, Callihan," I mumble when he climbs back up my body and kisses me.

He plants a kiss on each cheek before he presses his lips to mine. The musk of what he just did clings to his beard and I taste it on his tongue. "Told you my ego wouldn't be bruised."

He's so sure of himself. He always has been. It shouldn't make me want him even more.

"What about you? Think I can rock your world off its axis too?"

He grins into our kiss. "So not only did I prove you had nothing to worry about, I rocked your world."

"I should've kept my mouth shut," I grumble back.

"Apparently I made it impossible for you to do that. And I'm about to do it again."

He hefts me over his shoulder in a fireman carry and bounds for the stairs like the house is burning down around us.

I smack the flat of my hand against the curve of his ass, but he just laughs. I give up and grip the cotton of his t-shirt just above his hips.

He stops just inside an open doorway and lets me slide down his body. His cock pulses against my stomach, and I'm standing on his feet. "Look up," he says.

When I do, my breath catches in my throat. He has a mural on his ceiling. The first image I notice is one of a girl on a swing, her feet pointed toward a blue, blue sky, her head thrown back in laughter. There's the outline of a boy looking up at her. His face is covered by the shadow she casts, and his hands are clenched at his sides. But you can sense his fierce longing for the girl in every line of his body.

As my gaze sweeps over the rest of it, I have trouble finding words. Every single scene is one of our history.

"You painted us," I can hear the ragged edge of tears in my voice.

"Because I knew you'd come home some-day. I hoped I could show it to you and you'd know that there's always a place here for you." He thumps his fist against his heart.

The man is just as sentimental as the boy was, but there's one big difference. He's not afraid of what he feels and he's not waiting until it's too late to let me know.

I keep my eyes on his and pull the tangle of my t-shirt and bra over my head. "One of us has too many clothes on," I tell him as I slip a hand beneath his waistband.

"Easily fixed."

He tugs his shirt up and tosses it behind him.

His body wasn't carved by a gym. It was carved by checking fence, and climbing scaffolds and taking the tires off tractors. When I flick his abs, they're like granite.

He has a single tattoo winging over his right shoulder. When I bend close, what I see makes me want to cry again. It's a tiny bumblebee. I glide my fingers over it.

"When did you get this?"

"The week after I turned eighteen."

I gape in astonishment. "But that was six months before we graduated. And you started dating Cindy Houlihan that same month. And asked her to prom."

"I was a dumb kid and even though I was brave enough to get the tattoo, I wasn't brave enough to show it to you or tell you what it meant. It's only ever been you for me, Bumblebee. You're it."

"The whole time, I thought everything I felt was one-sided."

He gulps and grabs my hands. His thumbs stroke over my knuckles and he drops a kiss on my forehead. "It was never one-sided, Cassidy." His lips brush my throat. "Never," he breathes over my collarbone.

He's so sure of this. That this is the right time and the perfect place for there to be an us.

"I might not stay."

He lifts his head, his expression solemn. "I know. But I can't resist you anymore. I'll take what I can get."

He unsnaps his jeans and slowly unzips them. When he pushes them over his hips, his cock is right there. There's a drop of cum leaking from the head, and he wraps his hand around the length. His clasp tugs it toward his navel and he throws his head back. His jaw clenches when he does it again and the veins in his muscled forearm ripple with the movement.

There's not enough air to breathe. Not in this room. Not in the entire world.

My whole body bursts into flame. Like the fireman carry was justified and the house really is burning down around us.

"That's what you've been hiding?" I croak. "No wonder the girls on the cheerleading squad fought over you."

"The only one I ever went out with was Cindy, and we never went this far."

"Then it was based on rumors that were true all along."

"Crawl up onto my bed, Cassidy. On all fours, your ass in the air so I can smack it for all these questions."

My mouth drops open. He strides forward and puts his finger underneath my chin. "You heard what I said."

I swallow my astonishment and clamber onto his bed. I drop my face to my arms so I can watch him.

His expression is savage as he stalks toward me. It's hard to believe he's the same man who painted a mural of our history on his ceiling. It's hard to believe he's the same guy who marked his body with a permanent reminder of his childhood crush.

I lose sight of him when he stops behind me. When I feel the sting of his hand on my butt, my body jerks in surprise. He smoothes his palm down my spine, and then over the spot he just claimed.

That's how I feel. Claimed.

I hear the crinkle of a wrapper and I know he's putting on a condom.

I didn't even have to ask. I'm on shots to regulate my dysmenorrhea, but I would've insisted on protection for him too.

Just another way this is different. Just another way he's different. Conscientious and commanding at the same time.

He thrusts in all the way to the hilt and I shudder. I can feel every ridged inch of him when he wraps his hand around my hip, pulls out, and plunges forward again. It's exquisite torture and I can't stop myself from writhing in response. My hips are going to bear the imprint of his hold, like a brand on my skin.

"Mike," I wail, and he increases the pace. "Come for me, Cassidy. Let me feel that tight little pussy grip my cock so I can make it mine."

He's growling like he'll never get enough of me. His hips ram against me and he yells, "Fuck, yeah."

I feel him spilling inside me and his hold on my hip relaxes as he slumps over my back.

"I'll get something to clean us up," he mumbles like he's exhausted. "Just gimme a minute."

"I'm kinda hungry," I admit as my stomach rumbles. "And I've never had a guy cook for me."

We're laying in his giant bed after the second go-round. He rolls me onto my back and pins me to the mattress. "You finally screamed my name," he smirks down at me.

The first time cemented his ego, and he'll be insufferable now he proved his skill isn't a fluke.

"Pretty sure you screamed mine too, Callihan." He didn't exactly scream it, but he was groaning it like I was the last morsel on earth and he was a starving man.

He had a stash of condoms in his nightstand, and I'm trying to stamp down my jealousy. I wonder how often he does this and how many women have seen the mural he painted on the ceiling.

He lifts my chin with his thumb. "Stop."

"Stop what?" I ask defensively.

"Stop wondering, Cassidy. I can smell the smoke and see the wheels turning."

I want to cross my arms over my chest and act like I don't know what he's referring to. "I'm not wondering anything."

"Yes, you are. I bought those condoms after the first night. When I pinned you behind the velvet curtains. No other woman has been in this bed. No one but Brady has seen the mural. That blob of brown paint in the corner by the door is his version of a horse."

"Brady's the only one that's seen it?"

"Yes. And he has his own bedroom because he wanted bunk beds. I can't imagine anyone in this bed with me but you. Come to

Thanksgiving dinner. Brady will be there. And my parents would love to see you. Even Derek's been asking when I'm going to bring you around. You and your mom don't need to bring anything but yourselves."

"I can't believe your annoying little brother has been asking about me."

He folds his hands behind his head, a pensive look on his face. "He's different. Ever since he got back from his last tour five years ago. He finally started going to therapy when he became a deputy sheriff two years ago."

I lay my hand on his heart because I hear the worry and concern in his voice. "Is it helping?"

He shrugs under my touch. "I can't tell. He's better at controlling his anger. But it's hard to tell what he's feeling. And he goes through women and hard liquor like he's trying to banish his demons."

"I didn't think there were that many single women in Willow Creek. Less than ten thousand people live here."

"He finds them somewhere. Mom and Dad are worried too. Even though they haven't said anything to me, I can tell."

"Maybe it just takes the right person for each of us to find our way. Just watch over him and be his big brother when you need to be."

He kisses the top of my head. "You always were able to reel me back in when I started doom spiraling. Thanks, Cassidy."

My fingers trace circles over the trail of hair bisecting his abdomen. "You were always that person for me, too, Callihan. I'll talk to

Mom about coming over for Thanksgiving dinner."

⊰•⊱

When I unlock the front door of our farmhouse, I'm rumpled and carrying my shoes in my hand. I'm tiptoeing my way to the stairs when Mom's head pops over the top of the couch and scares me half to death. "There you are." She seems way too bright-eyed and bushy-tailed for two o' clock in the morning. "Come sit down and tell me all about it."

"Can I get a raincheck until tomorrow? I've been awake way too long today. He asked us over for Thanksgiving and I told him I'd talk to you about it."

Her face falls a little bit and I want to indulge her, but I want my sleep too. And the chance to ponder the ramifications of my actions tonight. My childhood best friend and I just tackled each other and went several rounds. And I toppled all the way in love with him.

She waves her hand in the air. "We don't need to talk about Thanksgiving. You can tell him we accept the invitation. Now, go get some sleep. But remember I want to hear everything in the morning."

Chapter Nine

Mike

Zane pulled me into his office this morning. "Mike, you need to buy her that piano. It's the grand gesture that'll get her to stay."

"What piano are you taking about?"

"The one that was in the estate sale just up the road from you. No one bought it."

"Why would I buy Bianca a piano?"

"Because she gave everyone there a concert on it."

"When did this happen?" She never said a word.

"Saturday afternoon. Molly Monroe called me this morning. She told me in no uncertain terms I needed to convince Bianca to take over the theater because she played like an angel." He shoots me a grin. "I told her I had my best guy working on it."

I throw my head back and groan. Now the rumors will be unstoppable. "No you didn't."

"I did. So you need to work your magic."

"We just had our first date." I can't hold back the smile.

He smirks. "Looks like it went pretty well."

"Yeah. It went pretty well."

He grins. Leans back in his chair and crosses his arms. "I knew it. Taren and I made a bet, She said Bianca wouldn't give in so easily. But I said I knew there would be a sleepover. Looks like I was right."

Taren and Zane's bets against each other have become almost legendary in this town. Sometimes they bring their entire circle of friends into it too, or every single person in Willow Creek.

I roll my eyes and cross my arms as I lean back. "I should've known you'd make Bumble Bee and I one of your stupid bets."

"Bumble Bee?" He guffaws. "That's what you call her? What kind of a nickname is that?"

"It's what I used to call her when we were kids."

"You have to think of a sexier nickname than that. Even something as generic as sweetheart would be better."

I shrug. "She doesn't seem to mind."

His eyes light up. "So you've called her that in bed?"

"Dude, I am not talking to you about what happens in my bedroom."

He gives me a smug grin. "You don't have to. Your face is telling me everything I need to know."

"Whatever," I tell him as I stand, because there's such a thing as too much meddling. "I have to go supervise stringing the lights across Main Street. I'll think about buying her the piano." I give him a salute and his laughter trails in my wake.

***

I just finished hanging the lights and the wreathes on all the town lamp posts, and I should go home and take a shower. But I need to see her and make sure she isn't freaking out about what's happening between us.

When I enter the church vestibule, I hear her.

Her voice stops me in my tracks – just like it did all those years ago. I lean against the wall and close my eyes.

She's right, she doesn't have the range she did back then. But her singing voice has this husky contralto undertone I can't get enough of. She's singing *Just You Wait* from *My Fair Lady* and her Cockney accent and delivery make me smile.

When her voice trails off after the last note, I start clapping. She whirls around, and she looks nervous. "I didn't mean for you to hear that. It was terrible."

"You're selling yourself short. It was magnificent."

"No, it wasn't. Broadway is like Shark Week and I already left a trail of blood in the water."

"Your voice might be different, but you still sound incredible." *You're still incredible, I want to tell her. You still stop the breath in my lungs and make me believe in things like fate and love and happily ever after.*

"What's phenomenal to your ears is mediocre to the ones that matter."

"My ears don't matter?"

She huffs in frustration. "That's not what I meant. I meant that your ears are untrained and you probably don't even notice the inconsistency."

"Why do you want to go back if it's so cutthroat? You have nothing to prove."

"That's not true. I have something to prove to myself. And to everyone who told me I'd never make my way back into the spotlight."

"You shouldn't care what they think." I don't know why it matters so much to her. It never did before. At least not when I knew her.

"If I can't do this it means the last twenty years mean nothing. What if I fade into obscurity?"

I scoff. "Now you're being ridiculous. Your voice is immortalized on dozens of cast recordings and solo albums. You have twenty-five million followers on the streaming app."

"But what if that isn't enough?"

"Not enough? You've built a career that's its own legacy and you're the most famous graduate of Willow Creek High School. Your not enough is more than most of us can even dream of."

"I can't just leave it all behind."

I want to shake her for being so stubborn and oblivious. "You can. People do it all the time. If beating yourself up like this doesn't bring you joy, you shouldn't do it. Tell them you changed your mind about your big comeback and they can fuck off."

She twists her hands in front of her. "Staging a comeback was all my idea. My agent said I should just retire gracefully."

"So you don't actually have to go back?"

"No. I don't. But I want to."

"You still want to?"

She tips her head and smiles sadly. "I do. You're weakening my resolve, but I want to make sure the people that deserve to be brought down a peg get what's coming to them."

"It sounds like revenge is what's moti-vating you, not the need to prove some-thing."

"Honestly, it's a little of both. After I had my voice surgery, my understudy convinced my producer I couldn't handle the part of Eliza."

"*My Fair Lady* was what you were cast in?" It's the one part she's always wanted.

"Yes, and you know what that role means to me."

I nod. I do know. She sang those songs incessantly. I know all the words as well as she does. Even twenty years later.

I walk forward and tilt her face into the palm pf my hand. "If you go, I'm not letting you forget about me like you did the last time. I'll come to you whenever I can and now there's such a thing as cell phones and Facetime."

She blinks up at me, her eyes full of unspoken promises. "Okay," she agrees.

Chapter Ten

Bianca

MOM'S ONCOLOGIST PULLS ME aside while she's still under.

"You have a very worried look on your face, Bianca. I promise I have welcome news, this time."

I relax a little, because Dr. Shumaker has always been open and honest about my mom's prognosis and what we should expect. I take a deep breath. "Lay it on me."

"The cellular degradation is slowing down, and I think the chemo's working. I have every confidence your mom will beat it this time too."

"So she'll go into remission again?"

She gives a soft smile and nods. Tears pool in my eyes and I grab her hand. "This is welcome news."

I've been preparing myself to say goodbye. I've been regretting all the years I wasted and all the times I let her convince me she didn't need me here.

<hr>

Me: I think I might stay in Willow Creek.

The bubbles pop up then disappear, and I can tell my best friend is typing something. Even though she moved back to Ohio seven years ago, we text or talk almost every day.

Cheri: I need to see your face while you're telling me this.

Me: So Facetime?

As soon as I send it, my phone starts ringing. When I connect, she's there. She still has stage make-up on, her cheeks bright red and her eyeliner a dark smear across the tops of her cheeks. There's a glass of red wine in her hand.

"Are you sure you want to stay there? You used to complain about it all the time."

"That was almost twenty years ago. It's nothing like I remembered."

"What about him? Is he anything like you remembered."

I try to be nonchalant. "Yep. Just bigger."

"And hotter too. He's all over the town's Instagram page."

"You stalked him?"

"Duh. Someone has to watch out for you. What if your old flame turned into a serial killer?"

"The things I want now are very different from the things I wanted back then. But thanks for always having my back."

She takes a gulp of wine. "Especially Mike Callihan, right?"

I sigh. "Yeah. He's always been something I wanted. I just didn't always think he'd be good for me."

"So you think he'd be good for you now?"

I blush. "Maybe."

Her eyes widen. "So that's what changed your mind. Spill, Bee."

"I'm not ready to tell you everything, yet. Give me some time. I called to talk about something else."

"Something more fascinating than a re-union?"

"So the town is buying the old theater in the middle of town. They want to turn it into a playhouse and a performing arts hub."

She takes another swig and drains her glass. "What's that have to do with you?"

"The town's marketing director asked if I'd be interested in running it."

She carefully sets down her glass on the table beside her before giving me a stern look. "What about your comeback?"

"I don't know if I still want it."

"Deep down there has to be some part of you that still wants it. Even if it's the teensy-weensy part that wants revenge on Amelia."

Amelia was my understudy and she convinced our director I wasn't going to recover my voice in time for opening night. I had the chance to finally play the character I've always wanted in the Off-Broadway revival of *My Fair Lady*, and the kid I always thought of as my mentee stomped all over it and took my place. It was that Bette Davis movie *All About Eve* come to life.

I brush my hair behind my ears. "What she did was underhanded. But I don't know if getting my revenge is worth leaving mom here by herself again."

Cheri's expression darkens. "You don't think she's going to beat it this time?"

"It's not that. There's a good chance she will. And I don't want to squander any time we have left."

"You know I won't judge you. That's why I came back here. I just didn't have a Mike Callihan pining after me."

"Am I crazy for considering the offer? You keep telling me community theater is a thankless job."

"You're not crazy. I love it, so I would never call you crazy. But it is thankless."

"I'll let you know what I decide. I might need a crash course."

"You'd better let me know soon – because I need details about your love life since it's like the Sahara Desert over here. The same seven guys keep popping up on my Tinder and Bumble apps."

"None you'd consider dating?"

"Are you kidding, me? Hell no. I'm pretty sure one of them is half my age. One is my old science teacher and he wasn't appealing then. I can tell from his picture that his ear hair is out of control. The other ones aren't much better. No thank you. I'll just live vicariously through you."

After we hang up I feel better about the possibility of staying in Willow Creek.

Mike knows Mom had her last treatment yesterday and she'll still be weak, so he left room for us to pull up right in front of his parents' house. He's opening the passenger door before I even manage to get out of my seat, and my heart swells when I see him on one side and a little boy on the other side I assume is Brady.

My new boyfriend flashes a wink and a grin over his shoulder as he and his son help my mom up the stairs. I trail behind them, bemused but unsurprised. He knew taking care of her first would mean the most to me.

I'm sitting on the porch with a glass of cranberry punch while Mom watches the parade when Brady comes outside.

"Can I sit beside you? I think the floats are weird and I need somebody to talk to."

"What about our dad and your uncle?"

"They're talking about work stuff."

Brady isn't what I expected. He's a smart alecky eight-year-old who has his dad's dimple and ornery grin.

"You can sit beside me. Hand me your drink so you don't spill it." He hands over his plastic cup.

Once he's settled, he peers up at me. "Are you the girl my dad painted all over the ceiling? You kind of look like her." He asks with a wrinkled nose.

I hold back my blush because it'll be a dead giveaway. "I don't think so. Your dad and I knew each other a long time ago, but I just moved back to Willow Creek."

Brady looks skeptical. "So the pictures could be of you. My mom calls this place podunk and says she doesn't understand why anyone wants to live here. My uncle Derek says she's just bitter because he gave her a speeding ticket."

"Sometimes people that didn't grow up in small towns don't appreciate them."

"So it's kind of like some of the gross stuff my nana makes for Thanksgiving dinner?"

"Your nana is an excellent cook. I'm sure nothing she makes is gross."

Brady scoffs and wrinkles his nose again. "You haven't tried her weird stuffing. My mom makes the cornbread kind that comes in a box. Nana makes hers from scratch and she uses *oysters*."

"There are lots of people who make oyster stuffing. But if you really don't like it, you should tell your nan. I bet she'd make some cornbread stuffing too."

He sighs. "I don't wanna hurt her feelings. So I pretend to like it and feed it to Fred when no one's looking."

"Who's Fred?"

"He's Nana and Pop's really old bulldog. He'll eat anything."

I smile, because Mike's dad has always had a bulldog for a pet. He always said he was obligated because he was from Georgia. "How do you know he'll eat anything?"

"He eats everything I give him off my plate."

I smile, because I bet Mike did the same thing. The screen door creaks open, and he strolls out. Like his ears were burning because I was thinking about him.

"Did you teach your son to give the stuff he doesn't like on his plate to the family pet?"

He grins sheepishly. "I would never do something like that."

I shake my head at the two of them. "It'd be much easier to tell her when you don't like something."

Mike and Brady share a smile. "We'd never do anything to hurt her feelings."

"The two of you are hopeless. That's exactly what your son said. You know that she probably knows you're sneaking stuff to Fred, right?"

"No, she doesn't notice."

"It may not seem like she notices, but trust me. She notices. Moms and nanas have a sixth sense about that kind of thing."

Brady's face falls. "I'd better go apologize and tell her the truth."

Mike ruffles his hair. "She won't hold it against you, bud. She loves you."

After he scampers off, Mike takes the vacant seat and throws his arm around my shoulders.

The trees in the distance are in full color, and even though the air is brisk, it's not unbearable. I snuggle into my fleece jacket and nestle my head against his shoulder.

"This is nice," he murmurs against my hair. "Almost as nice as waking up with you."

"It is nice," I agree. The weight of his arm around my shoulders feels like home, and I like how I can feel the seam of his jeans against mine when he pushes us off and our legs brush together.

"So tell me what you're thinking, Cassidy."

"That I should have known it would be like this."

His lips brush the crown of my head again. "Like what?"

"Like this. Easy and flawless and belonging."

"Belonging? You mean like all the pranks we played and the crap we put each other through when we were kids was all leading up to this? Yeah. I always knew this is how it would be. Belonging."

Mike's dad steps onto the porch, and I'm seeing the man sitting beside me twenty years from now. Jim Callihan's head of hair is still mostly dark, and his beard has an equal amount of salt and pepper. His broad shoulders are covered in a green flannel shirt, just like the one Mike's wearing.

I turn to Mike. "Did your mom make all of you wear matching shirts?"

I can't hide my delight, and he rolls his eyes. "Yep. Brady refused to put his on until we actually get ready to take the annual family picture for the holiday cards. And Derek will be here when his shift is over at four. He knows better than to show up wearing anything but what Mom picked out."

Jim shakes his head. "My wife is a force to be reckoned with. Just as I suspect you are, Bianca Cassidy. You were a holy terror when the two of you were kids in each other's back pockets and I bet you haven't changed much."

I shouldn't be surprised his dad remembers me. He bore the brunt of our pranks enough times, and got us out of some scrapes without telling our moms. I smile over at him. "Not on the inside I haven't."

He smiles back. "Don't let this knucklehead keep you away so long next time."

Mike chuckles. "Knucklehead. Really, Dad? How do you know I was the one keeping her away?"

Mr. Callihan shoves his hands in his front pockets and rocks on his heels. "Son, you should know by now that things like that are aways our fault. I'd let the two of you finish catching up, but your mom sent me out here to tell you the meal's ready."

Mike stands and tugs me into his arms. We hug for a minute before we follow his dad inside.

Mom gives me a pointed look when she sees our clasped hands. I want to shake my finger at her, because I can tell she's plotting something. Her smile gets even bigger when he pulls me under the mistletoe and kisses me like I'm all he's ever wanted for Christmas. There are a lot of oohs and ahs, and Brady's commentary, "Ooh, gross Dad."

Chapter Eleven

Bianca

I'M STILL SHOCKED THE Donaldson twins haven't ruined anything by now. Last night was the final dress rehearsal and Jerry Donaldson looked rapt when Suzie Danzig lifted the baby Jesus from the manger. Maybe they haven't done anything because the ringleader of the two is crushing on Suzie. Baby Jesus is a doll, because none of the new parents in town trusted the town scamps not to perform some disappearing trick with their kid. But maybe they shouldn't have worried – one of the twins is definitely smitten.

A couple of the angels stepped on their hems and the shepherds keep complaining about the bathrobes they're wearing. Farrah and Sarah are helping me with last-minute wardrobe malfunctions, and Emma provided the snacks. No icing on the cupcakes because she said it would be just another mess waiting to happen. The kids don't seem to mind, they're scarfing them down like there's no tomorrow.

Taren walks in, pecks me on the cheek and hands me a bouquet.

"What's this for?"

"My husband is over the moon that you're here, and he's been in a good mood for weeks now. It's a little thank you from me to you for that."

"I'm sure his mood has nothing to do with me."

"It has everything to do with you and what he thinks this will do for Willow Creek. He's excited you're thinking about restoring the Majestic too."

A dark-haired man in a blazer and jeans slides his arm around her waist. "My wife is right, you've been good for Willow Creek so far, Bianca Cassidy."

He holds out his hand and I take it as he pumps enthusiastically. "I'm sorry I've been too swamped to introduce myself before now, but I'm Zane Reid."

I smile when Taren affectionately rolls her eyes. "I know who you are, Mayor Reid. It's been my pleasure, though I admit I was daunted at first by the prospect of directing and producing tonight's show."

He grins. "I know it'll be great. Trevor told me he still can't believe the change you've wrought in the Donaldson twins."

I bend toward them so I can whisper. "Can I tell you a secret?"

They both nod.

"I think they're competing for the privilege of being Suzie Danzig's boyfriend. I heard a rumor she told them she won't be seen with bad boys."

All of my friends burst into laughter.

"She'll change her tune when she hits fifteen. Mark my words," Sarah observes. "I see
it every day at Willow Creek High." She's
the high school science teacher and girls'
soccer team coach, so she's speaking from
experience.

***

The play didn't go off without a hitch. One
of the choir members started bawling in the
middle of *Hark! The Herald Angels Sing*
because she peed all over her robes. And
the Donaldson twins aren't completely re-
formed, because they lined the steps going
up to the altar with strategically placed bub-
ble gum, and when Joseph's foot got stuck
he almost fell right into the manger.

But it's over and we received a standing ova-
tion and the kids are all beaming now. I'm

making my fourth bow when Mike bounds onto the stage.

"Folks, if you'll stay seated, we have a surprise." He waves his hand toward the back of the theater, and two lines of kids start walking toward us. They're high schoolers and half of them have their instruments.

He turns to me. "Bianca, just because you aren't going back doesn't mean you should give up on Eliza Doolittle. I know it's not Broadway, but I found you an orchestra and a choir if you'll sing for us."

The unmistakable notes of *The Rain in Spain* surround us and I want to give him a kiss he'll never forget, audience be damned.

"Will you stay up here with me while I sing it?"

He lifts my hand and presses a kiss to my knuckles. "It'd be my honor."

He's there to hold me steady, just like he has my whole life. He makes me brave. As soon as I open my mouth and the first stanza soars out, the crowd quiets. I close my eyes and grip the hand of the man who promised to take care of me and set the music free.

The church is quiet when I finish and I open my eyes, ready to face the judgment. But then the whole audience rises to its feet and erupts into applause and catcalls. Mike hauls me to his side. "Told you," he says into my hair.

Later that night, as he spoons me from behind after he made me sated and sleepy from his very energetic, very bossy lovemaking, I flip around so I'm facing him.

"I made a decision tonight."

"You did, huh?"

I can tell he's trying not to get overexcited or get his hopes up.

"Yeah, I did. I decided Willow Creek is enough. I decided you're enough. That you've always been enough and I'm not going to find enough anywhere else."

"Does that mean you're staying?"

"Yes, Callihan. It means I'm staying."

He rolls onto his back and pulls me on top of him. "Does that mean you're moving in? So we can make love every night underneath our story?"

I nudge his nose with mine. "Not right away. I've only been back for six weeks."

"That wasn't a no."

"That wasn't a no. It was a later."

"I'll take it, Bumble Bee," he murmurs against my lips.

Chapter Twelve

Mike

It's Christmas morning. The piano was delivered about an hour ago, and the girl I've loved my whole life will be here soon. I have a ring pop in my pocket because I haven't had time to shop for the real thing and I'm still afraid she might tell me no. And I know the ring pop will remind her of when we were kids and make her smile bright and wide.

The ring pop was Brady's idea. I ran my intentions by him first to make sure he was okay with them.

"You should get her a ring pop. I think she'll like it since you guys have known each other for so long. I knew you were gonna ask her by the way, when I saw you guys kissing under the mistletoe. She's cool. But tell her just because I'm okay with her marrying my dad that doesn't mean I'm okay with being in one of those plays." I laughed and ruffled his hair. And told him I'd make sure to tell her.

When she knocks on the front door, I open it. I'm still shirtless and in my bare feet because I've been running around trying to get things ready in time. We usually end up tackling each other within five minutes of being alone, so I don't think she'll mind.

Her eyes flare and she slides her hands down my bare chest after she pops up and plants a hello kiss on my lips. "Merry Christmas, boyfriend."

I scoop her up to give her a proper kiss. "Merry Christmas, girlfriend."

When we're both breathless and I'm dying to be inside her, I pull away. "I need to give you your present before we get carried away."

"You can give it to me later," she pouts.

"Nope. Come on," I tell her as I grab her hand and pull her behind me. "It's in the family room. And you have to close your eyes. I'll take you to it and tell you when you can open them."

"You've already given me so much," she protests. "Things I don't even know how to measure."

"But those weren't Christmas presents, Cassidy. That was me giving you things you needed. Like self-confidence and help taking care of your mom. I want to give you things you don't need."

I stop in front of the bay window. The piano's in the center of it, looking out over the gardens. Brady helped me wind garlands and lights around the bench and there's a candelabra with one of my mom's Christmas doilies sitting on top of the instrument. "You can open your eyes now."

She does and then turns to me in confusion. "Since when do you have a piano, Callihan?"

"I don't, Cassidy. You do. I heard about your impromptu concert at the estate sale through the town rumor mill. I had one of my college buddies tune it for you."

She squeals and throws her arms around my neck. "Can I play it?"

"I was hoping you would. But that's not all of your presents." I take a deep breath for courage. "Will you sit on the bench?"

She obediently sits down, the piano at her back. Her eyes widen when I drop to one knee.

"I know I haven't said the words, Bumble Bee. But I'm yours. I always have been. I love you because you're my other half and the one person who makes me whole. I love you because you always take my dares and you make me laugh and your voice is the song in my heart. I love you now even more then I did when we were eighteen, and all I want for Christmas is you. Will you marry me someday?" I hold out the ring pop.

Her mouth curves into a smile and she slides off the bench so she can throw her arms around my neck. "Yes, Mike Callihan, I'll marry you. Because you're all of those things to me too. And even though I love the piano, you're the only thing I really want for Christmas too."

Sneak Peek at Twelve Days and Twelve Nights, a Willow Creek Christmas Story included in the Wreck My Halls Anthology

Chapter One

Ness

Alex McIntire and I have this thing every year. At least every year for the last three years.

During the advent countdown to Christmas, right after the town tree-lighting, we bang it out everywhere we can, at every possible opportunity. Like screaming tomcats in an alley. We both like it raw and dirty and hard with no strings attached and the other fifty weeks of the year we act like we're nothing more than casual acquaintances.

But I know what his callused palms feel like against my skin. I know he likes it when I wear red lingerie. I know he likes the smell of pumpkin spice and burns the chili on his stove when he's distracted.

I know he makes me laugh as much as he makes me want him. This year, it feels different.

When he grabbed my hand and pulled me into the shadows last night, it felt like he was taking me home. Like nothing would ever upset me again. Feeling this way is dangerous. He was married to our class president for twenty years and he was devastated when she left him. He's trying to raise teenagers on his own, and this little thing we do is a secret we keep from everyone else in our lives.

It's a secret I start a countdown for the day after Thanksgiving. A secret that makes me smile while I'm sipping my morning coffee or stuck on bus duty.

But he's changing the terms.

There was a plain envelope in the mailbox when I got home yesterday. No address. Just my name scrawled across the front. I almost threw it away.

I recognized his handwriting. It's the same script on the inner curve of his forearm- the tattoo with the names of his kids twining around a rose.

He's a gruff single dad with two teenagers. He has a beard and tattoos and a hard body I've licked every inch of. But he's never ripped off his armor and bared his poet heart.

I didn't even know he had a poet's heart. Until now.

And I don't know what this means. Is he giving his heart to me on this piece of yellow, college-ruled paper? Is christening every inch of our spaces with the slide of skin

and sweat and longing no longer enough?

Acknowledgements

A huge thank you to all of you who pre-ordered, to the series organizer, C.H. James, and to my amazing team of ARC readers.

A very special shoutout goes to my first five readers, Whitney, Iesha, Raeann, Katlyn and Mya, who literally read Mike and Bianca's story as soon as it dropped – no matter how busy their lives were.

It's the season of gratitude and I am very aware that I wouldn't be able to do this without the support of my family, especially my husband, my friends and all of my incredible readers.

About the author

Andrea is a 2023 HOLT Award Winning Author who's had characters begging her to tell their love story since she was thirteen years old. She's learned to manage her ADHD, but it can still get really chaotic sometimes because her characters are from different worlds, different eras and different genres.

She lives on a peaceful farm with her spouse and loves nothing more than connecting with her readers. You can subscribe to her newsletter via her author website, at andreajenelleromance.com or join her Facebook group, The Willow Creek Wantons.

Welcome to Willow Creek

<u>**The Willow Creek series consists of interconnected standalones that can be read in any order.**</u>

<u>**No Regrets, Willow CreekBook One**</u>

A brother's best friend, enemies to lovers, small town romance.

Once upon a time he was her brother's best friend. He taught her to put the worm on the hook. He let her follow them around. But they grew up and he broke her heart when she needed him the most. Now he's back and he owns half of her business. And he wants a chance to redeem himself. Taren wants her family's heritage orchard and cidery to survive and Zane's going to help her make that happen and win back her love.

Can she trust him with her family's legacy and her heart?

Trigger & Content Warnings: I have experienced the loss of immediate family members and have done my best to portray grief. For those who are triggered by scenes about the emotional turmoil of death and the effects it has on those who must carry on, and those who are particularly sensitive to the grim real-

ities of elder care, especially dementia and Alzheimer's, please read with caution. This book also contains four very explicit intimate scenes and several instances of what could be considered foul language throughout.

No Surrender, Willow Creek Book Two

A rivals to lovers, forced proximity, small town romance with social anxiety rep.

Their meet cute is a three-legged race. She suffers from social anxiety but will do anything for her friends. She's a former soccer star who craves peace and quiet, ice cream, Guardians of the Galaxy and 90s alternative music. He's a hot former real estate mogul who grew up in foster care and wants to make a difference in the world. He's a gearhead who loves his motorcycle, has a wicked dart game, and crochets to settle his mind. Sarah is content with her life. The last thing she needs is a distraction. Especially a distraction like Blake Armitage, the sinfully delicious man who is Willow Creek's newest savior. But now he's turning up everywhere. He's a rival coach and her newest neighbor. And he clearly wants a much more intimate relationship.

Trigger & Content Warnings: MC with social anxiety, references to gun violence, the death of a sibling and being raised in the foster care system. This book also contains three very explicit intimate scenes and several instances of what could be considered foul language throughout.

<u>No Promises, Willow Creek Book Three</u>

A winter holidays, best friend's brother, stern brunch daddy hero, suspense sub-plot, small town romance...

He's her best friend's brother and they've been flirting for five years.

As much as Emma wants to climb Trevor Hayes like a tree, he's the last thing she needs in her life. She's building a life in Willow Creek so she can stay under the radar. She's in hiding, and she doesn't need the town's hottest law enforcement officer snooping around.

When her past catches up with her, he won't let her say no to his protection. She's determined to resist him until they get stranded together in the season's first freak blizzard.

Trigger & Content Warnings: suspenseful plot, PTSD. This book also contains

five very explicit intimate scenes and several instances of what could be considered foul language throughout.

No Shadows, Willow Creek Book 4

A best friend's sister, second chance, military, small town romance.

Dex and Marianela met in the middle of a war zone and spent a magical weekend together. Three days later she was assigned to his combat platoon as their field medic and he found out she was his best friend's little sister.

They had to act like they'd never met.

Tragedy strikes and they're separated. Almost nine years later she's the new emergency room physician in Willow Creek. He's never stopped thinking about her and all the things he should have done. She can't forgive him for the things he couldn't say.

They both fight personal demons on a daily basis and are working through the trauma of their combat experience.

Will the shadows between them keep them apart or push them together?

Trigger & Content Warnings: This book features a couple who meet when they are both serving in Afghanistan. Although I'm a veteran I did not experience this deployment. I have spoken with those who did to capture their feelings, emotions, and the way their deployment affected them and their families. This book features what maybe described as emotionally intense combat scenes, the death of a sibling, and main characters struggling with PTSD and

adjusting to life with a prosthetic limb. There are at least five scenes of explicit, open door intimacy, and the occurrence of foul language throughout.

<u>No Doubts, Willow Creek Book 5</u>

An age gap, grumpy vs. sunshine; single dad; starting over small town romance.

Alaric is a driven astrophysicist who's only in Willow Creek so he can finish his book and give his twin daughters the chance to reconnect with their aunt.

He doesn't have time for the inconvenient attraction aroused by the sassy, always glass half full niece of his eccentric innkeeper.

Farrah is in Willow Creek because it's her last resort. She's putting her life back together in the wake of the pandemic and she thinks her aunt's houseguest is arrogant and annoying.

When they meet in the rain, she think he's condescending and he thinks she's a hot mess.

It's anything but a perfect match.

Trigger & Content Warnings: Off page death of a parent; off page reference to death of a spouse; struggles dealing with grief, job loss and difficult relatives; public gossip and attempted shaming about family history. Several instances of foul language as part of normal conversation. THIS IS WHAT IS CONSIDERED AN OPEN DOOR ROMANCE. THERE ARE AT LEAST FIVE LENGTHY SCENES DEPICTING EXPLICIT INTIMACY.

<u>No Excuses, Willow Creek Book 6</u>

An opposites attract, grumpy heroine vs. golden retriever hero, age gap romance.

She grumbles at him and feeds him fried baloney sandwiches for dinner. He does everything he can to make her smile.

Roxie Greene is a ball buster, and River Montgomery isn't used to it. When everyone warned him about signing up to be her farmhand, he assumed they were exaggerating. They weren't.

Roxie Greene does everything she can to keep River Montgomery at a distance because she knows he's working on her lavender farm as a last result and he'll leave like everyone else. She's been hurt too many times, and she's not letting her golden retriever help get close enough to disappoint her again.

River Montgomery is just trying to claw his way back from the darkness and desperation and pain and addiction that destroyed him. He might only be twenty-eight, but he's learned life is short and you have to do everything you can to make it sweet. He wants to take all the brittle pieces of Roxie Greene and glue them back together. If she'll let him.

Trigger & Content Warnings: This book features a female main character who suffers from endometriosis and who has experienced both infertility and miscarriage. It features a male main character with an opioid addiction he is recovering from. The female main character is reclusive and distrustful because of the way she has been treated by the town and people in general. There are four scenes of explicit open door intimacy and foul language sprinkled throughout the text.